Crump Redivivus

Neil Godsell

the voidery aperture

First published in the United Kingdom in 2016
by
the Voidery Aperture

www.thevoideryaperture.com

ISBN 978-0-9954812-0-6

1

Lomas

It was Bettina's idea, but I was as much to blame. For going along with it, I mean. For going along with it, looking for Crump, that old fraud Crump, affecting interest in his mundane disappearance, if he'd disappeared at all, whatever had happened to him, all that, and trying always to be meticulous and vigilant when the body, the physiological thing, the flesh, is predisposed to ruin everything, by which I mean one's plans.

Bettina

It's fair to say he encountered problems. And it's true that I was to blame. I had an idea about looking for Crump, and so I put that idea to Lomas, thinking it might perhaps do him some good, and to my surprise he went along with it and kept on going along with it and wouldn't stop going along with it, and that's why I was to blame.

Lomas

It's fair to say I encountered problems, such as technical problems, and personal problems too, including the eighteen months I had to spend in bed with only intermittent access to my box file. It was the strain of the extra work, in part, that put me there, my socks and old shoes by the bed, or slightly under it, and then of course my coat, the oldest of all, apparently vigilant on the stool beside the bed, the box file younger than the socks, its contents older than what contained them, everything suitably unassuming, just as waiting objects should be, as you'd expect.

Bettina

I think what I said was, Crump knew his business, knew his

subject, which had something to do with the nature of human existence. He'd gained insights which were said to have the potential to transform the life of any given person, making that life not only bearable but pleasant and even rewarding. Lomas had issues, which is what they used to call problems; he needed a project to give him a sense of direction or purpose. Crump had gone missing, and people were worried. So I suggested it, looking for Crump.

Lomas

He'll put you right on a thing or two, she said, assuming you can find him. Having something to keep you busy will do you good. Yes, it'll be good.

Saoirse

He came looking for me at the pub where I was working. Up on the moors. When I arrived for my shift he was lurking there, in the car park, in the rain. He looked a bit dodgy. I assumed some aging pisshead or pothead or smackhead had taken a wrong turn down in the valley and ended up miles out of his way and then decided to take in the view. He seemed to be scrutinizing me, actually. I brushed past him and went inside. I had to change some barrels and light a fire with logs and coal in the lounge. When I opened up, he was still standing there, in the car park, in the rain.

Lomas

I started where the information ended. Two years before, I'd been there looking for a person called Adele, who knew about Crump, or was supposed to know about Crump. The box file said so.

Lomas [box file]

Adele chose the venue, a former weaving shed or something. Black stone, moss between the slabs, a yellowish lichen encrusting the masonry, the whole of it colluding in the fiction that it's always been like this, that some kind of ancient natural order governs this dark and rain-scoured outpost of 'tradition' with its foursquare setts and cracked old slates and lintels. Already I'm bored, and my inspection of the place has induced a slight but niggling headache. Sweat trickled down my back when I walked round the car park. Sky and moors, an impression of greasiness, the sky a yellowish smear from which a few pale swellings, discernibly clouds, loom aimlessly, not moving, while the moors below dissolve in their own acid. None of which has much to do with me. The sky a smear, the moors just moors. Adele is late.

Lomas

All in all, I was glad to be rid of him, this former self, this peevish and fanciful interloper defiling the backs of old envelopes, planting corruption in the archives, trying to stall me, trying to ruin my chances of resurrecting the project which he'd failed so ignominiously to complete. Even his manner of writing the findings up was flawed. I hoped he hadn't allowed his peevishness to colour the way he'd spoken to Adele, if he'd got round to it. I might have, or I might not. I couldn't remember.

Saoirse

He just kept talking about Adele, going on about that, all does she work here, when did she stop working here and where did she go when she left. Which wound me up and predisposed me to find him offensive, even after it became clear he wasn't a junkie or a drunk.

Lomas

She took against me even before I'd opened my mouth. This much was obvious when she rushed from her battered old hatchback, making her way towards a yard at the rear of the pub, and happened to glance at me, quite briefly, in disgust. And something else. Perhaps resentment. Yes, a finely tuned combination of resentment and disgust. The expression seemed familiar, though she didn't.

Saoirse

He just sat there by the fire, drinking and steaming, probably thinking up his questions, how to put them, who best to put them to, me or Tania. Out of the two of us, she was clearly the more approachable one, but that day she was being even more annoying than usual. She'd been watching a show about corpses, how to dispose of unwanted corpses. She was telling me about that.

Tania

They said all you need is washing powder, loads of it, but it has to be biological. Non-bio doesn't work. What you do is, you put the body, the person's body you want to dispose of, in the bath or whatever and fill the bath completely full with powder. And they showed you – using a pig, I think it was. It turns the flesh into this kind of weird loose scum, and you just scrape that off the bones and wash it away. So all you're left with is a skeleton, and for that you need sulphuric acid or something. You dissolve it, and you're done. It's like, no way! I couldn't believe it. But apparently that's what you do.

Lomas

Observing Saoirse's clipped, perfunctory responses, I saw it again, still finely tuned but more subdued now, eyes and mouth, that combination of resentment and disgust, the constant pressure of which would not be inconsistent with an aptitude for hatred. Eyes and mouth weren't in the notes, that combination of resentment and disgust wasn't in there either, nor the name on the brushed steel badge she wore, the name by which her colleague, Tania, called her. There were two names on two badges, and none was Adele. So while Saoirse was bringing in pies and things from the kitchen, I asked Tania what I needed to ask, and got nowhere, other than learning that she thought Adele a good name for a baby girl, though Heidi and Amelia were her favourites at the moment. On my behalf, she put the question to Saoirse, who was arranging the food in a grubby plastic display case on a shelf to one side of the optics, and who flatly denied knowing anyone of that name. When I asked them both about Crump, I got no further.

Tania

He looked faint. Not well at all. As if he hadn't eaten in days. And we'd already had one case that week of someone who'd come in and had a drink when they were obviously ill. That ended badly.

Lomas

I felt I could manage a packet of crisps, but nothing too fancy, none of your chilli vanilla or honey-glazed mint and prawn, just salted crisps, plain salted crisps, and maybe afterwards a bowl of soup and some bread. Except you couldn't trust the bread, the rolls and sandwiches were stiff with age, you could see, just as the sallow pies resembled uprooted cobblestones, slightly green and probably dangerous. Food from a tin was the answer, supposing they had it out back. Crisps, and afterwards tinned food. I wondered if Tania would agree to open a tin of marrowfat peas for me, and heat them up in the kitchen, and allow me to consume them in the bar; she seemed the sort who might well do that, offered some money, spoken to courteously, with money.

Tania

They should really stay in bed when they're like that, not go around boozing like they're kids. They make a mess, and then everyone suffers. But I felt sorry for him, this guy, he seemed quite nice. That's why I tried to help him out. So I asked Saoirse, did we know this bloke, this girl, the ones he asked about, their names, whatever they were, but she was actually quite off with me about it, verging on rude.

Saoirse

I don't do names. People come to the bar, I serve them, and that's it. I don't do names.

Tania

We'd already ended up throwing a load of stuff on the fire, what with the mess they made and the smell there was after they'd gone. He slid his hands down the back and stuck his fingers inside, and well, you know, you could just see. I couldn't handle it, not on a Tuesday afternoon. What made it more bizarre was this Pierrot kind of costume she was wearing, though it might have been pyjamas. She was only two days out of hospital, they said.

Lomas

And then quite late, about half past ten, as I was preparing myself to leave without a result, and having been told that there were no marrowfat peas in a tin, she caught my eye and nodded almost imperceptibly towards the door to the car park, so I went outside and waited by her car. It was raining still, I'd taken several hours to dry out sitting by the fire, but I was soaked again in minutes, and when she came splashing across to let me in, however long it was later, half an hour, maybe longer, and the light came on in the car, I could tell she was none too pleased by the state of my trousers and my coat.

Saoirse

You'll get the upholstery wet. It'll stink for the next six months.

Lomas

You should have told me to wait by the fire.

Saoirse

And make it obvious there was something going on?

Lomas

There isn't something going on. What do you think is going on?

Saoirse

I should have put down one of those vinyl things, those seat-covers people with dogs use.

Lomas

I'd be quite content to walk, if you prefer.

Saoirse

So now you're insulting my driving as well?

Lomas

As well?

Saoirse

Don't push it.

Lomas

She was glaring straight ahead and working the gearbox with unnecessary violence, braking hard and then accelerating harder, driving recklessly, the unlit road, the sudden bends and drops, and all those potholes, all those shattered verges crumbling into space.

Saoirse

You're steaming the windscreen up. For fuck's sake, make yourself useful.

Lomas

The cotton vest she tossed that landed in my lap smelled faintly of perfume, tinctured with engine oil and foist. I rolled it up and wiped the glass, but when it came to doing the driver's side the elongated strokes were quite a strain because of my feebleness, my convalescent feebleness, and though I tried to keep a steady hand, not wanting to block her line of vision, still I managed to provoke some hissed expletives, which not only came as no surprise but also induced a strangely comforting sense of inurement. We were descending into the valley, and soon there came traffic, lots of traffic, prompting some hazardous overtaking, quite alarming but only partially responsible for the rapid dissipation of that comforting sense of inurement, which gave way to a familiar kind of dread as we were inducted into a network flow of renovated commercial estates and gaping floodlit retail parks, two burning cars in a yard, a grinning youth extracting a sizable gun from his underpants, three females playing a game of dare with the firearm, never quite touching it, giggling nervously, first lunging, then recoiling, and a drive-in pizzeria where some youths were struggling to bundle a hooded figure into the boot of a big saloon. Saoirse's attention remained on the road, a sharp cut left into a cobbled lane that skirted a disused railway, someone lobbing a weapons-grade firework into the path of the car and Saoirse driving over it, unflinching, more lanes, rumble strips and speed humps and an underpass, two further detonations, then a block of flats that overlooked a canal. Here we stopped and she confronted me.

Saoirse

So then. What's all this about Crump?

Lomas

What? You tell me.

Saoirse

You'd like to know.

Lomas

That's why I waited in the rain.

Saoirse

Are you always this flippant?

Lomas

I'm not being flippant.

Saoirse

You're being flippant, obtuse and unpleasant. And if you don't tell me about Crump, this conversation's ending right now.

Lomas

I'm just looking into it. Finding things out.

Saoirse

What things?

Lomas

Don't know yet.

Saoirse

Christ. You lying bloody shit. You're working for that little bitch Adele.

Lomas

I don't actually know her. I might have done once. But not any more.

Saoirse

I heard you ask for her by name.

Lomas

Well, yes… to find out who she is and what she knows.

Saoirse

About Crump? What about him?

Lomas

I don't know yet — like I said. But I'm wasting my time here. I'm repeating myself already. It's no good, that. It's a definite sign of decline.

Saoirse

You need to wait here.

Lomas

What?

Saoirse

Stupid bastard, *fucking wait here.*

Lomas

She was out of the car and dashing up the road, and only now that I saw her mule heels buckling in puddles at the kerbside did I realize how unsuitable her footwear had been for driving. Not only that, she'd left the engine running, the offside door was open, rain was soaking the driver's seat, the dashboard was beaded with droplets and apparently I was meant to sit and wait. Or was it a test? I felt obliged to show some initiative, so I turned off the engine, got out and locked the car, tugged on both handles to check it was locked, then hurried after her, pausing only to stuff the box file down the front of my coat to shield it from the rain.

Saoirse

He just barged in, the insolent prick, he just barged in, came up and hammered on the door, the cheeky sod, all stupid questions and politeness, fake politeness, bumbling stupid insolent wanker, all an act of course, all sorry but what about this and what about that, demanding this, demanding that, and I just lost it I suppose.

Lomas

We were rolling on the floor like a couple of wrestlers in a tangle of electrical cords and telecom cables, Saoirse, who'd initiated the struggle, hissing threats and accusations, how she'd bloody well fucking well show me, bastard well coming up here to gloat. I had to defend myself against her gouges and blows, and yet the more she struck and scratched at me, the more my compassion increased, and so I tried to restrain her by hugging her, pinning her arms to her sides, a strategy which served only to intensify her frustration, as I could tell from her manner of thrashing her legs and twisting her neck and trying to bite my ear, and when I thwarted her by pushing her head down firmly against my collar-bone she redoubled her exertions with her legs, attempting to kick my shins and knee me in the groin. Instinctively I trapped the offending limb between my knees, and once our legs had interlocked she began to grind the base of her pelvis against my thigh in a fashion that seemed to me to be less than entirely combative, and then I thought I sensed a kind of mutual surprise, as though quite suddenly, against our will, we'd recognized an unlikely convergence of interests. Foolishly I allowed this idea to engross me, and next came that surge of discomfort I hadn't expected to feel so early on after my illness, and while I was busy feeling it Saoirse attempted to brain me with a six-plug trailing socket.

Saoirse

Sorry about that. I overreacted. It's something I do.

Lomas

The bedsitting room was a mess, an absolute tip. Tousled bedclothes on the mattress in the corner. Dresses, underwear, phones, that snarl of plugs and cables, books with covers ripped off, torn magazines and posters on the floor. More clothes piled against the skirting boards and packed around the bottom of the window to absorb the water leaking in at the top of the frame and seeping from the coving on the ceiling. Three old portable tellies stacked on a low metal stand, an obsolete indoor aerial balancing on the topmost. I was slumped in the single armchair, still in my shoes and soaking coat. Saoirse had brought a cold wet flannel to act as a compress for my head. I sipped a large medicinal brandy while she leafed through the box file, smirking to herself.

Saoirse

These notes are useless. You couldn't find anyone from these. Least of all Crump.

Lomas

He's a man who knows how to stay hidden?

Saoirse

He had this way of dropping out of things. He started off with some firm ideas about life and what to do with it, but equally he was honest enough to admit when he'd made a mistake, and since he was happy to swap a failing idea for a stronger one, or what seemed at the time like a stronger one, certain people tended to see him as a loser or a crank. And there were others who encouraged it, that habit he had of changing his mind and trying all sorts of new things and ideas. They tried to turn him into something or someone he wasn't.

Lomas

That was how she broached the topic of Juniper.

Saoirse

On the basis of some flimsy association during their time at university, she made herself indispensable ten years later, when her tits were beginning to sag and all the other political radicals had moved on to deal in derivatives or sell tracts of deciduous woodland to foreign gangsters and there was no-one left to fuck. I suppose she squatted over his face and used her flaps to pluck a coupon for a third-world village goat from between his teeth, or whatever these crazy old hags do to show that their earth-goddess credentials are still in order. No doubt she saw her hairy old undercarriage as a portal into the past, the eternal feminine, all that nonsense, a mystical passageway back to the age of youthful idealism they'd shared, the world that was lost; you know all the clichés. Within months they'd got themselves shacked up in her cottage out in the sticks. Living the dream in this filthy old pigsty with no electricity other than what they could get from her re-conditioned fair-trade solar panels, burning their own dried poop to keep themselves warm in winter. They convinced themselves they were saving the world by growing their own asparagus and getting blind drunk every night on home-made wine from the shitty old raspberries they picked from a bush out the back. God, it was revolting.

Lomas

How long ago?

Saoirse

What?

Lomas

When did this happen?

Saoirse

I don't know – maybe ten years ago, maybe twelve. You start to lose track. But like I said, they had this old connection, loonies on the march together, stitching up banners to smash the moneyed hegemony, ranting in pubs as a form of non-violent direct action, and that went back ten years further still. He'd pretty much given it up when I knew him, but he talked about it sometimes, the state of the world, the probable imminence of catastrophe, the ethics of refusing to participate, and when he talked like that I always got the feeling he despised me ever so slightly – not that he'd say. Because for me, the whole political thing, it really had no meaning. I was younger by five years; it might not seem much but I think it made a difference to how we viewed things. I was resigned to mass extinction but I didn't want to talk about it, or think about it even; we were sliding into the shitter and there was nothing I could do except to keep on blotting it out and doing the various things I had to do for money until it all became too obviously atrocious – that, and making sure I had enough pills and booze on hand for the overdose, the precautionary overdose. When I said as much, he accused me of being a nihilist, though he couldn't quite find it within himself to take issue with me, not really; either he recognized I was right about the world, or he could see me all too easily in the bathtub with the handful of pills and the booze, and that made him sad, too sad to argue. We were going through a bad patch at the time, and not long afterwards Juniper hauled the old dugs and flaps back onto the scene to give him a radicalizing post-feminist re-education. So that was that – until we met up again, years later.

Lomas

You swapped back?

Saoirse

What?

Lomas

You swapped round again?

Saoirse

I see they didn't employ you for your tact.

Lomas

They?

Saoirse

What happened was, I bumped into him, not literally, in the car park at the hospital. And then, in a room – not this room – a

14

nicer room – the room where I was living at the time – we took our clothes off, most of our clothes, and did as much as was physically possible.

Lomas

This room you were living in – was it within the hospital grounds?

Saoirse

No, it was two miles from the hospital, it was a decent size, and actually it was ideal for two people who wanted to do as much as was physically possible with their clothes off. That's what we did. And soon enough Juniper got wise to what we were doing, and started the counterattack. I think she'd been expecting them to grow old together, or should I say grow ancient together, a sloppy old witch and a withered old druid mutating into an oak tree together; no way was she giving that dream up without a bitch-fight. So she set about ripping him off, pretending to suffer from this degenerative mystery illness, which meant Crump had to take on the role of long-term carer, something he wasn't especially good with – and it was me, of course, he came to for relief. And when she realized that playing the bedridden cripple was proving counterproductive, she resorted to something crazier, or at least more melodramatic, disappearing from the cottage in the middle of the night.

Lomas

He started hallucinating?

Saoirse

No, she really did vanish.

Lomas

But you say he wasn't good with it. He cracked up?

Saoirse

He started to crack.

Lomas

It's just there's evidence he began to suffer hallucinations or something. That's how I interpreted it, the evidence. He was hallucinating.

Crump [box file]

We had stopped on the way from nowhere to a nastier part of nowhere. We needed fuel but there was none. The garage forecourt was overgrown. Hemlock and willowherb towered from cracks between uneven concrete slabs. The pumps just stood there, seemingly stunned by their own obsolescence, pockmarked with rust. The shop was deserted, and the fuel tank was not in the van. Whereas we used to have a car, we now had a van, and the fuel tank was not where it was meant to be. The fuel tank was in my lap. Clumps of sod were jammed inside it. I sat cross-legged with the fuel tank in my lap and tried to unblock it with a screwdriver. I extracted a lump of moss and threw it away. It was as though I'd scored a victory. Only I hadn't. Shame overwhelmed me. From her stretcher on the forecourt, Juniper watched. She was enclosed in a white canvas body bag. Four leather straps around the body bag and the stretcher held her secure. The body bag was unzipped at the top, allowing her to move her neck when she felt like looking around. She watched me picking out clumps of grass from the fuel tank and throwing them off to one side. She neither approved of what I was doing nor condemned it. Her face was expressionless. The distinction between life and death was of no interest to her.

Saoirse

He was under a lot of pressure. They were sleeping in separate rooms by then. A carer and his patient don't have sex. Or aren't supposed to. He was woken up by the sound of a woman coughing, but it seemed to have come from downstairs. That's why he assumed that he'd been dreaming. There was no way she could have managed the stairs by herself, not with her degenerative mystery illness. So he drifted off back to sleep, as any normal person would. Next time he heard it, the coughing, it seemed to be coming from further away, outside. He heard a car door slam and an engine starting. Next day she was gone, and so was their car.

Lomas

Did she come back?

Saoirse

Apparently not.

Lomas

Did they ever trace the car?

Saoirse

Burned out in some quarry. That's when the police got involved, and actually they suspected him for a while. They looked at her medical history. From that they concluded she wasn't physically capable of going downstairs unaided with an overnight bag and driving off in the car. So Crump must have murdered her. It didn't seem to occur to them that she might have been making it up. I think he blamed me for what happened. He started avoiding me, at any rate, and soon I started getting all these really bizarre reports about his behaviour. How he'd sit in a pub and chant to himself in whispers, like he was learning something by rote or doing revision for an exam, and how he stopped turning up for his part-time job stacking shelves, and how he'd go on these long-distance bike rides, always at night and always on unlit country roads, no lights on the bike. I was concerned and I wanted to help, but he wouldn't see me. And then I heard about how this person called Adele had got involved. She'd known him before, when they were in their early twenties, and by the time I got the

full story he'd disappeared. That's why I reacted the way I did
when you mentioned her earlier. It was like I was being used, like
you were using me to appropriate him in someone else's interests.

Lomas

So you knew her? This Adele, you actually knew her?

Saoirse

No. I told you. I just took the job in that godforsaken pub as her
replacement, after she stopped turning up for work. I'm not
waiting for him, I never was the type to wait for anyone, but it
bothered me that we didn't part on good terms. I wanted to find
out what had happened and I thought he might go back there.
And somehow I've been there ever since.

Lomas

And Crump? Any theories?

Saoirse

Decomposing in some dosshouse.

Lomas

You don't see him as a man of the road, an outdoorsman?

Saoirse

A pox-raddled flagellant, sprawled in a ditch and spewing abuse
at innocent bystanders.

Lomas

That's not consistent with the image I've constructed of him.

Saoirse

What would you know? Your file's rubbish, you've haven't got a
chance of tracking him down.

Lomas

So you said.

Saoirse

But if you think it would help, I could show you some of the places we used to go. I've got the day off tomorrow. I'll take you, if you're willing to fill up the car.

Lomas

She had this peculiar method of working her way up the mattress, inching backwards on her bottom with deliberate thrusts of her heels, occasionally pausing to enjoy or test out a posture – raised on one elbow, for example, or reclining on one side. It was only when her head got as far as the pillows that she settled, stretching out on her back with the quilt gripped under her chin. Did she manoeuvre like that every night, or only when entertaining strangers? Would she undress beneath the quilt, would there be clothes, a change of clothes, already bundled under the pillows, in preparation for the morning, and if so, would they be un-acceptably creased? I didn't ask her; she appeared to have fallen asleep. And since she hadn't asked me to leave, I helped myself to another brandy and tried to get comfortable in the armchair, using my overcoat, still wet, as a makeshift blanket. There was faecal material smeared all down the back. It looked like a seagull's. People called them that; the proper name was herring gull.
Herring gull.
Larus argentatus.

Crump [box file]

It is currently denied me, if that's right, there is no quarter, what I mean is, where it is, it gives no quarter, in the form, I mean, of what it might have been, or what it was, or what it used to be, what action, in the form I mean of action, in the form of remedial action, it is currently denied me.

Lomas

Pounding music woke me up. The walls were vibrating and so was the ceiling. Saoirse's mattress was unoccupied, the bed-clothes had been thrown aside and left in a rumpled heap, and I could see that there was no-one in the bathroom, so I filled the tub, undressed, and then submerged myself in the water, keeping my nose and mouth a little above the surface and my ears a little below it until the cacophony came to an end about two hours later. There was no towel in the bathroom, but I didn't want to go rummaging round in the bedsitting room in case Saoirse re-appeared and took offence, so I just crouched there in the tub and dripped dry, shivering, brushing out bits of grit, exfoliating grit, from under my toes. Once dressed, I warmed myself through by finishing Saoirse's brandy. It was mid-afternoon; the rain had stopped; a few rivulets of water still were dribbling down the walls, but their pace had slowed. I hadn't updated Bettina for weeks now, and couldn't help thinking that the right thing, the appropriate thing, to do would be to make some form of contact – nonverbal contact – without delay. I tried the mobile phones on the floor, but three were locked, and two were broken, while the sixth provided access to a menu but had no network coverage anywhere in the flat. I wondered how Saoirse had spent her day off, and where she was now, and why she hadn't kept our appointment.

Saoirse

I still had a life. I don't think he grasped that. I wasn't just waiting around for some miserable sod, some loser from the past, to wade back in and make everything good again, everything rosy. It never had been.

Lomas

When the music started again, just after midnight, it was louder than during the day, the volume inducing an immediate, un-accountable surge of dread that slackened my bowels before I could reason my way out of it, the visceral shame of sensory subjugation. I suppressed the need to defecate, but the nausea simply moved on and within seconds I was vomiting, heartily vomiting, into the toilet – Saoirse's toilet, where poor Saoirse must squat and vomit every night unless she had earplugs to grant her some peace. Would earplugs work? How did she stand it? Maybe she didn't. Maybe that's why she had to get out. And maybe I should get out too. And in a sense, of course, she'd offered me her car, the use of her car; she'd placed her car at my disposal, not even asking for the keys, which were still in my pocket. All I needed was to fill up the tank and go, to find some place such as a chip shop or kebab van whose proprietor would look the other way while I helped myself to some rancid vegetable oil, and the car would be mine to drive. I'd have to speak, there'd be unknowns, it might not work, but I could try. I felt it might work.

2

Lomas

The cottage was deserted when I arrived. Most of the windows had been smashed in. Someone had used a can of aerosol paint to spray a large ejaculating penis on the front door. There was no trace of the solar panels Saoirse had mentioned, only gaping holes in the roof where tiles had slipped. I gained access by forcing the door of a rickety porch at the rear of the house, and found the interior stripped almost bare, although the bathroom sink and toilet were intact. As the water supply seemed fine, I decided to stay for a couple of days. I could get myself cleaned up, mend the holes in my socks, and finish the crackers and spreads I'd bought along the way. I was exhausted and couldn't face driving back to Saoirse's in a car with an insistent pull to the left and all those whining idiosyncrasies. She hadn't been keeping the service schedule up to date, that much was clear.

Juniper

I was just digging up a few plants with a view to saving them from the bulldozers, and that was when I noticed him skulking about at the side of the house. In strictly legal terms we were trespassing, both of us were, but the cottage was so remote the developers hadn't bothered with proper security: no patrolling heavies or guard dogs, just a low wire fence and the usual corporate signage – which was how, I suppose, he'd managed to get inside and spend a couple of nights on site with no-one realizing.

Lomas

I looked out and there was this woman in baggy old clothes and she was digging up what had probably once been a flowerbed. When I ventured outside, she smiled and said hello in a fond, familiar sort of way, as though she knew me.

Juniper

He seemed harmless enough, a lost soul.

Lomas

And then she chocked the spade in the earth and put her hands on her hips and arched her back and took a long deep breath. Perhaps what Saoirse said had coloured my perceptions, but both the long deep intake of breath and the outbreath that followed struck me as having, or affecting to have, a yogic sort of precision and control.

Juniper

Actually, you couldn't see most of the signage. It was overgrown with lilac. You wouldn't have guessed how neat and tidy it had been, both gardens had been, when we'd been living there. Round the back, of course, it had always been more functional, more of a working market garden, but the front had been traditionally ornate: flowers and shrubs and all the rest of it, a monkey puzzle and heathers. We even had orchids. And it was the orchids I'd come back for, because in the turmoil of moving out it had completely slipped my mind to dig them up, and now I was settled in my new flat I had this balcony and I thought a couple of orchids would look good there. I could sit in the evenings and look at them.

Lomas

There was a trolley on the driveway. Four big pots inside. The first was full of ground elder, the second had nettles, I think there were dandelions in the third, and she was planting what looked like hogweed in the fourth.

Juniper

He asked me how I planned to get the orchids back. I had this trolley, a sort of trailer for pedestrians, with a tug-rope so I could pull it along behind me; when I told him I was using that, he asked how far to your flat, and I said twenty-five miles, maybe thirty, and he offered me a lift. I said no thanks, it seemed a terrible waste of fuel, I didn't want all that extra pollution on my conscience, and besides, he must have lots of more important things to do. But he was insistent.

Lomas

You owned a car yourself once.

Juniper

I ran it on vegetable oil. When I could.

Lomas

Me too. This one's full of chip fat. Incidentally, how easily does a car ignite on vegetable oil?

Juniper

Ignite?

Lomas

Supposing you want to set it alight and leave it burnt out in some quarry.

Juniper

I was unwell at the time. I didn't have any alternative but to burn it out in a quarry.

Lomas

The pots could fall off. The plants could be damaged or even killed. If you pull them on your trolley.

Juniper

It seemed a fair point. He seemed to care about my plants – not in a pushy way, but with genuine concern. So I accepted. The car was parked at the end of the lane; he backed it up and we loaded them in.

Lomas

As we drove to her flat, she explained about gardening as therapy.

Juniper

It takes you out of yourself. Connects you with something bigger. All the great cycles of life, the eternals of recurrence and rebirth. They've done studies. Just a couple of pots can really make a difference. You can draw a huge amount of positive energy from a garden.

Lomas

What did Crump make of that idea?

Juniper

It hardly matters.

Lomas

Because of what he did with Saoirse, while you were ill?

Juniper

There's no resentment — not on my side, not any more. It's just a case of diverging paths. The end of our time together was dreadful, but now I just view it as part of the process that delivered me into my present state, which isn't exactly perfect but it's better in terms of calm and equanimity than the state I was in before. It's just like organisms have to wither and die before an ecosystem can enter its new season. With his corrosive rational scepticism, Crump could never have followed me on that path. It was only by doubting rational scepticism myself that I started to open up a possible way to recovery; even then, it was a struggle to reject what I'd been brought up to believe. Medical science couldn't help me. The doctors, for their part, couldn't agree on what was wrong with me. Myalgic encephalomyelitis had gone out of fashion by then; when I mentioned it, they didn't want to discuss it. They thought it was polymyositis, then they didn't, and then it was multiple sclerosis, then it wasn't. Every so often they'd go right back to the start and tell me it was clinical depression. Meanwhile I was sleeping eighteen hours a day and taking half an hour to crawl across the room to piss in a bucket. It was sheer desperation that pushed me towards alternative ways of healing. I had no desire to tell Crump about that journey. I thought if he knew, he'd only contaminate it. As you can tell, we'd fallen out pretty badly by then.

Lomas

Because of Saoirse?

Juniper

That didn't help. Whatever you think of her, though, she wasn't entirely to blame. In a way, it was my fault. We'd always said that our relationship was conditional; we thought we could avoid the petty hang-ups that start to drag people down when they throw in their lot as a couple. So right at the start I made it clear that if I died while we were together, he should go straight out there and find another woman and not feel the slightest guilt about doing so, especially if it was just for meaningless sex. And later, when I became ill, and it looked like the illness might be progressive and incurable, I told him that if it took me ages to die, he shouldn't feel any pressure to stay. If you love someone, why make them watch you die? It's the cruellest thing in the world. Even if he did choose to stay, I promised not to hate him if he found someone else to have sex with. But when he started seeing Saoirse again, for a while I actually lost my faith in life. It was the fact that he'd gone to Saoirse – specifically Saoirse.

Lomas

She's got quite a temper.

Juniper

That's not the worst of it, not by a long chalk. They'd had this fling when he was twenty-nine or thirty, and he was still in a state of shock, still recovering from the ordeal, when we finally got together the following year. So I'd seen what she could do to him. If he'd gone for some desperate old slattern he'd found in a bar, the type who'd peel off her nylon knickers as soon as look at a man and wouldn't feel degraded when he didn't bother to say bye-bye next morning, I might have felt differently. But Saoirse, with their history? Didn't he have any self-respect? Of course, she couldn't let him cheat on me discreetly. She was the sort who always had to be pushing the boundaries, making a bloody great public statement. Getting him to take her to the hospital like that, while I was flat on my back like a living corpse in the house and he was meant to be doing the shopping. Actually, he might have got away with it – only I knew someone at the hospital, and when I was in for tests one day she happened to mention seeing him in the corridor, pushing an outpatient in a wheelchair. His younger sister, she assumed. Except he didn't have a sister, younger or otherwise.

Lomas

I wasn't entirely sure what to say, but it was fine, she just kept talking while I concentrated on driving. The traffic was bad, and it was raining.

Juniper

What got me most was the fact that her medical problem wasn't even life-threatening. Not just that, it was entirely self-inflicted. Later on, you see, I started finding out about her. I thought it would do me good to know the worst of it, so I could channel all my anger, get the whole lot out of my system, and then start the healing process. Some of the stuff I learned was unbelievable. She'd always been desperate to break into the media, and her latest attempt to get people sitting up and taking notice was one of those mission programmes – the mission being, in this case, to find out why women insisted on doing such bizarre and frankly pointless things to their bodies. How she managed to talk her way into that, I don't really know – maybe talking didn't come into it – but there she was, pestering all these tearful women who were so depressed and self-conscious about their fannies that the only dignified option was to spread their legs on camera while some bloke with surgical gloves and a greasy moustache went poking round and Saoirse asked questions in a sympathetic voice. She looked at their problems, she looked at the ethics, and after a certain amount of soul-searching she came out on the side of renovation. Hence the splendidly sordid climax: the intrepid presenter herself, shaved and splayed and on the slab, awaiting the cuts and tucks that would give her the perfect vagina. Live surgery was popular back then; I suppose in her mad way she thought that going under the knife would stand her in good stead for a career in investigative journalism. But something went wrong, there were complications on the operating table, the show was never broadcast and the production company went into administration, leaving Saoirse with a mangled snatch, a failed career and zero self-esteem but plenty of cunning, being pushed around the hospital in a wheelchair by a man whose life she'd ruined several years earlier.

Lomas

Even then, some aspects of Juniper's account struck me as implausible. Sensationalist and prurient, not to mention counter-intuitive. My first impressions of Saoirse seemed incompatible with this image of a failed full-frontal investigative reporter. Still, what did I know?

Juniper

You're probably thinking that what with her injuries, the betrayal was largely platonic. But no, it wasn't platonic at all. Once I was sure of her involvement, I went to work on him, I mean *really* went to work, and I got to the truth of it eventually. They'd been wallowing in the filth with each other for weeks. Which meant that now, instead of just staring at the ceiling, I could stare at the ceiling and go through all the things that you could do to a man and all the things a man could do to you in the temporary absence of a functioning vagina. Which, believe it or not, was instructive. Really, it helped me to move on. Could you turn down there, please?

Lomas

We descended into a tunnel, which levelled out quickly and then climbed back towards the surface, where four concrete tower blocks overlooked a quadrangle. The quadrangle was landscaped, containing a pond, some bushes, three hillocks and a tree. Juniper directed me to a parking bay on the perimeter, where we unloaded the first two pots.

Juniper

The lift was out of order. We had to take the pots one at a time, and then go back to get the trolley.

Lomas

The stairwell was unlit and smelled of stale urine and rotting vegetable matter. As we laboured up and down, she told me all about the latest trends in roof and veranda gardening. Her balcony was little more than two feet long by one foot wide, so we had to balance the pots with the dandelions and hogweed in them on top of the pots with the nettles and ground elder, jamming the rims against the railings on the one side and the concrete on the other. When everything had been arranged to her satisfaction, we sat on beanbags in the living room, drinking home brew.

Juniper

Once we were settled in and comfy and the conversation had stalled, he started asking about Crump's politics.

Lomas

It seemed like the appropriate thing to do. We'd had relation-ships and gardening and illnesses and surgery, so I asked about it, apathy and nihilism, all that, and actually how political was he?

Juniper

Well, it varied over time.

Lomas

He was more committed when younger?

Juniper

I think we all were – those who bothered to get involved.

Lomas

Yes, she mentioned that you were active in the same circles.

Juniper

She?

Lomas

Yes. Saoirse. Happened to mention it. Your shared political interests. A connection going back years before she met him. I got the impression that it rankled slightly more than she cared to admit.

Juniper

You're suggesting that he never really connected with her on anything more than a superficial level? Whereas he and I had this deep, indelible bond? What are you doing – trying to make me feel better?

Lomas

From one side of the beanbag she lifted a cat, or the mortal remains of a cat, a rigid thing with all four limbs sticking out and clumps of fur missing. At first I was a little embarrassed to look, it seemed so obviously dead, but then she pressed it to her face, and kissed the scruff of its neck, and laid it across her lap, and proceeded to massage it with lengthy, powerful strokes, occasionally lingering at the backs of the ears to tickle them, so that after a while the body appeared to relax, and I thought I even heard it purring faintly. It made such a soothing spectacle, I started to feel quite drowsy.

Juniper

I went on to tell him how I'd made my peace with the past and didn't bear any ill will towards anyone now, not Crump and not even Saoirse, and I hoped her vagina was better. That woke him up, the word vagina. He was obviously exhausted and he'd nodded off, just like that. Perhaps the home brew had gone straight to his head.

Lomas

The sudden realization that I'd almost tipped my beer onto the linoleum brought me back to myself with a start. Juniper, still stroking the cat, was smiling. You were saying, I said, about Crump's political views. His youthful enthusiasm, it waned?

Juniper

To an extent. Doesn't it always? Not that he actually sold out. He stayed a contrarian, a refusenik, to the point that he sometimes made running away from life seem like a high political principle. Which, in a sense, is how our relationship began – our relationship proper. We had this friend from university who'd bought a rural smallholding in France and let it evolve into a sanctuary or retreat for people who needed to escape – failed writers and artists, old Ranters and Diggers, assorted dropouts he'd known and feted over the years. Tadeusz Grody, he was called. If he liked you, he'd let you stay for next to nothing; all he asked was that you bought your own food and wine and cleaned the toilet before you moved on. I'd just crashed out of a misguided career in social work when Tadeusz invited me over. It was exactly what I needed at the time: that summer was beautiful, really beautiful. Crump turned up about three weeks after I did, and he was a mess. We spent a lot of time together; I suppose because we'd known each other before, it seemed both comfortable and slightly dissolute, as though we were breaking some kind of taboo. After Grody's place, we slummed our way around Europe for a few weeks. We wanted to try something with each other but weren't convinced it would be feasible, making a life together, a decent sort of life with minimal impact, minimal harm. We were drawn to the idea of buying a place in the French Pyrenees or somewhere – living quietly, growing our own organic produce, keeping a few dozen free-range chickens, that sort of thing – but of course we didn't have the wherewithal for that, we lacked the cash. I gave some thought to selling the house, but it had major structural problems; finding a buyer would have been an absolute nightmare, the way the market was back then. Even if I'd sold it, there wouldn't have been enough left over to subsist on until we got sorted out in France; no regular income, no fund for emergencies if the harvest failed or the chickens got lifted by foxes. I needed to get back to work, to find a new job, embark on a new career. As for Crump, he wasn't really up to supervising a large-scale building project. He was still having panic attacks. They started when he was with her.

Lomas
After you vanished, he didn't stay with her all that long.

Juniper
Well, there you go. I wasn't too bothered, by then, to be frank, in how he was choosing to fuck up his life. I was too busy –

working hard on my recovery.

Lomas

If I may say so, that went well. I mean, you look well.

Juniper

I've got my spiritual advisor to thank for that. He set me exercises – meditational sequences that concentrated my energies on the smallest of movements and gradually made them more sustained and ambitious. Before I left, while Crump was occupied with Saoirse and her wound, he'd talk me through them on the phone, or sometimes come over and give me guided meditations, until I was confident enough to take control of the process myself. It really worked. Within a few weeks I found my mobility vastly improved, and soon I could manage the stairs without help. But I had this fear that if I told Crump, or he began to suspect what was happening, then the illness would take hold again and I wouldn't get a second chance at self-healing. That's why my departure took the form that it did, a vanishing act in the night. I'd been planning it for some time, transferring money, laying false trails in advance; I'd booked a long-term residential place in a spiritual retreat, a non-sectarian community devoted to alternative ways of healing, but even Ken, my spiritual advisor, didn't know that. I mean, I knew they'd be able to track me down eventually, if they really put the resources in; I just wanted a few months' grace. It was only after I was back on my feet and starting to think again about selling the cottage that I found out Crump had disappeared as well.

Lomas

The last person he was in contact with was a woman called Adele.

Juniper

Adele?

Lomas

You knew her?

Juniper

We were friends. Crump had a thing with her in our last year at university. She was nineteen and rather fragile. After a year, they parted by mutual consent. It was amicable but sad. I liked Adele.

Lomas

Where is she now?

Juniper

I've no idea. She moved around a lot. From disaster to disaster, you might say. Crump helped her out from time to time. We'd get this panicky call and he'd go and try to extricate her from the latest catastrophe.

Lomas

You didn't mind?

Juniper

Not at all. Why would I? She was nice – quite the opposite of Saoirse. Do pass on my regards, if you track her down. And if you find Crump, please let me know. I'll give you my number. I'd be interested to see how he's getting on.

Lomas

How do you think he's getting on?

Juniper

Well, for the record, I think he's dead.

Lomas

How dead?

34

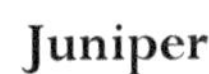

Juniper

I'm sorry?

Lomas

If you had to guess, how dead would you say he is?

Juniper

I'd say almost dead.

Lomas

You're sure of that?

Juniper

I hadn't really thought about it till now. But now you've asked, my gut response is that he's dead, or close to death. Or that he thinks he's close to death.

Lomas

One of her neighbours was using the party wall for penalty practice – had been, now, for six or seven minutes. The player, a man, sounded heavy and bestial, old enough to know better. I could tell it was a man because of the guttural roar of triumph that succeeded each whacking great thud.

Juniper

So, then. Why are you targeting Crump?

Lomas

I'm sorry?

Juniper

Why Crump?

Lomas

I'm hardly targeting him. I've never targeted anyone.

Juniper

Why him and not somebody else?

Lomas

There's a moral imperative.

Juniper

What does that mean?

Lomas

People valued his existence.

Juniper

You mean their happiness depended on him? Him, specifically him, and not somebody else? And that's why you're targeting him?

Lomas

I have my duties to perform. Searching for Crump is one of my duties.

Juniper

Will you be talking to his male friends?

Lomas

There's no point.

Juniper

Why not?

Lomas

They won't tell me anything.

Juniper

What's the matter?

Lomas

It's that football banging against the wall, distracting me. Sorry.
I should be paying closer attention.

Juniper

Crump, like you, was sensitive to noise. The back of the house,
which was where our bedroom was – or rather where it had
been, when we'd still been sharing a room – it took the brunt of
the prevailing wind, a screaming mad southwesterly. All the
window frames needed replacing, and the brickwork needed
repointing, but the money situation meant we never quite got
round to it. So the wind howled through the cracks, and often
the rain came in, and Crump just couldn't stand that. The
palpitations would start and the earplugs would go in, and next
he'd be rolling out a tarpaulin over the counterpane… Actually,
there was a storm the night I left, which probably worked out in
my favour. I made a racket, stumbling about.

Lomas

He wasn't wearing earplugs, not the night you left. He heard you
coughing.

Juniper

He went back to sleep?

Lomas

Unless he was never awake to begin with.

Juniper

You must have been terribly ill. I mean, it must have been awful
for you. I can sense it.

Lomas

I beg your pardon?

Juniper

Right from the start I had the feeling you were… sort of *convalescent*. What was wrong with you?

Lomas

Tachycardia. Cricopharyngeal spasm. And dysphoric hyperarousal.

Juniper

And your renewed interest in the enquiry is a pragmatic way of establishing continuity with your life before the illness?

Lomas

I wouldn't say that.

Juniper

Don't get me wrong. I'm not judging anyone. What you've chosen to do is a valid means of self-healing. It's only by coming to terms with the past that you can move on to something better.

Lomas

So I've heard.

Juniper

Are you all right? If that noise is distracting you, we could sit out on the balcony.

Lomas

I should be going. I have an appointment.

Juniper

Well. Another time, perhaps. Thanks for helping with the plants. I'll get you my number.

Lomas

While she was writing it down, I asked her about Grody's bolt-hole: which *département*, the name of the nearest village; was he still down there, or had he sold up? Having failed to acquire more pertinent information, I thought it a reasonable thing to do.

Juniper

I don't know why he asked about Grody. Mind you, the way he looked, I thought a few weeks out there might do him good.

Lomas

She'd been trying to draw a confidence from me, right towards the end. There'd been something deeper afoot than mere polite concern for the health of a fellow convalescent. Positing Crump as the primary motor of continuity in my existence seemed provocative; her insistence on the centrality of his experience to mine jarred with her own professed detachment from whatever course his life had taken since they'd fallen out. I wasn't convinced by her repeated claims that she'd laid to rest those things which had formerly hurt her. The more I thought about it, in fact, the less satisfactory our encounter began to seem. With her glib effusions of wisdom and goodwill, she put me in mind of those paper fortune-tellers children used to prize: the swift manipulation of facets and colours and symbols, the solemn chanting of the litany, the irrefutable proclamation when the chanting came to a close. And yet I'd found her pleasant to talk to. She had seemed personable and engaging. Maybe my judgement was at fault.

Juniper

I offered him cupcakes, home-made cupcakes, but he declined.

Lomas

Fifteen miles from the flat, I had to pull into a lay-by so I could vomit. It was a thin expulsion: orange bile laced with yellow, beery froth. A blustery wind played round the car, rocking the chassis on its springs and whistling distantly in the air vents. I found myself thinking again about Crump's depiction of Juniper, stretchered mutely on that deserted garage forecourt. It was difficult to credit the piece as a literal representation, but it made me feel uneasy. I should have checked with her. I should have sought verification of the account.

Lomas [box file]

We were on the Brittany coast. It was a quiet, sheltered bay. I had fallen asleep on the grass at the top of the cliffs. When I woke up I felt suddenly anxious. I was anxious regarding her whereabouts. She wasn't lying down or standing up or walking around on top of the cliffs. I crawled to the very edge of the cliff on which I'd been sleeping. The tussocks were crowding over the edge. I peered beyond the outermost tussock. I saw her swimming in the middle of the bay. Silver wavelets veered aside from her as she swam, a loose formation of glints like a giant rippling arrowhead. I didn't see how she could have reached the water alive: there wasn't a safe path down to the shore and the cliffs were far too high to dive from. The wavelets weren't wavelets at all but fish. The fish were lying on their sides. It was their scales reflecting the sunlight. The fish were dead, or probably dead; I couldn't be certain. My companion wasn't moving. She was swimming but making no progress. She was suspended in the middle of the bay. I wanted to help, but I was up on the cliff and she was down in the sea. All I could think of to do was to wait. And so I waited.

3

Lomas

According to the box file, Constance's flat overlooked a depressing expanse of broken glass, small animal bones, and nappies caked with excrement and blood. Access was gained through an alleyway lined with overflowing bins. Arriving, I found that my information was fundamentally accurate: fourteen apartment blocks, identically squat and boxlike, hunkered together around their communal square or courtyard, plenty of rubbish and plenty of ordure. I parked as close as I could to the exit.

Constance

The first time he came round to ask about Crump, the bailiffs had just been in to repossess my bed. I remember the screeching noise the legs made as they scraped along the ground behind the truck, and how the mattress, which they hadn't secured, slid free, and how they mustn't have noticed or maybe they just didn't care, because they left it, the mattress, lying in the square. I could have dragged it back up to the flat, I suppose, and tried to clean it up and gone on using it, but actually there was so much broken glass, so many used needles and so much dogs' dirt on the ground that pretty much straight away I decided it wasn't worth saving.

Lomas

They'd chained her bed to the tow bar of their truck. She was indignant in her brown-and-orange housecoat, doing her best to keep her temper as they laughed at her and blew cigarette smoke in her face. Just before leaving, one of the blokes — the one in the high-visibility jacket — stubbed his fag out on her sleeve.

Constance

It was the usual brutes, the two that always came, always stinking of pot smoke and diesel and sweat.

Lomas

She climbed up onto the bed and grabbed the wrought-iron bars of the headboard, and stayed there even when the truck began to move off. They must have realized, because they started playing a game with her, a game that consisted of trundling round and round the square with the bed slewing this way and that until it finally flipped its mattress into the filth, at which point she lost her grip, slid down, and tried to clutch at the springs but failed and got one ankle jammed in the bars at the foot of the bed. The driver slammed on the brakes; she rolled off onto the ground.

Constance

I'd been dragged round the square maybe half a dozen times before I realized there was a witness. Someone other than the neighbours watching, I mean.

Lomas

The driver was revving the engine and laughing at her as she struggled to get to her feet, and when she came running towards me the truck was right behind her. My back was against a high wall, which I assumed she wanted to climb, and guessing the driver wasn't committed enough for a calculated hit and run on a stranger, a stranger who wasn't dressed in a brown-and-orange housecoat, I just stood and cupped my hands and hoped I still possessed the strength to hoist a fully grown woman to chest height. But rather than leaping into the toehold, Constance grabbed my shoulders and frantically tried to scramble up my front; her slippers kept stamping down on my kneecaps as though they were rungs on a ladder, my hands meanwhile trying in vain to capture a foot. To our left was a prefabricated cabin. The truck had already stopped and gone into reverse; I sensed that the men were bored with their game and would soon drive away, but you could never be sure when it came to thugs in trucks going after women, so I pushed her into the cabin and flicked the light switch by the door.

Constance

It was embarrassing, being caught outdoors in my housecoat.

Lomas

Human excrement was spattered up the walls, the place was a toilet, I had my back to the door and still she was trying to scramble up my front. To keep my balance, I bent my knees and tensed my thigh muscles, such as they were, and then she clamped her legs around my hips, and then I put my arms round her back, and then she put her arms round my neck, and when she continued to slide down my front I took her weight by linking my hands beneath her buttocks. We remained like that for a moment.

Constance

Some of the local women, they'd go to the shops in their nighties or pyjamas, even take their children to school like that, the ones who went to school, but I was embarrassed, being seen like that, in my housecoat.

Lomas

When the noise of iron scraping over tarmac had faded away, I realized that Constance was having trouble getting her breath. Her torso was heaving, and there was a wet patch on my shoulder, which prompted the queasy apprehension that some basic, human response was required: a reassuring phrase of some kind, something gentle and platitudinous but not so gentle and platitudinous that it might be taken as an expression of sexual interest. Clearly there was a protocol to be followed – there was a protocol for everything – but since I hadn't been trained in the treatment of trauma and stress conditions, I didn't have any firm idea of what might be appropriate. So I tried instead to be practical.

Constance

The first thing he asked was whether I'd got the number of the truck so I could report them to the authorities. I told him there was no point. The bailiffs knew what they were doing, they always covered their plates with tape before they drove into the square, and the ID cards they carried were likely to be fakes. Besides, as far as the repossessions went, the law was on their side. I couldn't do anything to stop them; whenever I tried, I came off worse. To prove the point, I showed him my injuries from the time I'd tried to stop them taking my hostess trolley away.

Lomas

She lifted the hem of her housecoat, revealing a fresh pink scar on each knee.

Constance

It really upset me, losing that hostess trolley. I treasured it. And I'd had to order it specially. You couldn't really get them any more, not properly made ones, like they used to make. Lomas clearly sympathized, but he didn't really get it, I could tell; I think he took the view that losing a bed was the sort of thing that ought to put the loss of a mere hostess trolley into perspective.

Lomas

I can't remember what I said, but it made her angry. God, she said, that's such a sodding bloody masculine thing to say.

Constance

Actually, though, he was right. Losing my bed was a serious matter. They'd taken the sofa two weeks earlier, so I'd be sleeping on the bare floor, or in the bathtub, until I could sort myself out with a camp bed or an inflatable mattress or something. I decided to be stoical. After all, they'd done me a favour in a way. I was redecorating the flat, and the repossessions meant there'd be less to move around.

Lomas

Looking at the blood, and the sort of rubbish there was lying in the square, I said you need to scrub that out with a sterilized brush and some antiseptic.

Constance

I decided to be stoical, but I was probably still in shock. I asked him to give me a minute or two, which he was fine with, saying something about checking his box file in the car. I went inside and cleaned my wounds and put some plasters on.

Lomas

At first, when I went to the door, she seemed not to recognize me. The effort she'd made with her appearance, though, suggested that she'd been expecting someone to call. In place of the housecoat she wore a purple chemise made of polyester or viscose, along with an apricot pashmina. Sticking plasters covered the cuts on her wrists; her elbows, where the grit had gone deeper, were bandaged. She still had her slippers on.

Constance

What do you want?

Lomas

I've come to help you with the redecorating.

Constance

What's that on your trousers?

Lomas

Human excrement, I think. You must have got some on your slippers when we were hiding out in the toilet.

Constance

Slippers?

Lomas

Earlier. When we were hiding in the toilet together. Trying not to fall over.

Constance

Earlier...

Lomas

Look, I don't suppose you've got a washing machine, or a sink. If you've got a sink and some detergent, I'll clean them up. You know, my trousers. If you'll allow me the use of your bathroom.

Constance

I haven't got a washing machine, not any more. But I can get you a change of clothes.

Lomas

She showed me into the bathroom, where I got to work with the scrubbing brush and detergent, using the bath instead of the sink – partly for greater freedom of movement, and partly because I didn't want to splash diluted excrement where Constance brushed her teeth and washed her face. After several minutes, a bundle of clothes was pushed through a gap in the door. I heard her voice outside.

Constance

These belonged to a man I used to know. You might as well keep them. Don't worry, they're clean.

Lomas

Won't the gentleman mind?

Constance

I very much doubt it. He's not coming back.

Lomas

Is there anywhere I can dry the ones I've washed?

Constance

Sorry, the heating doesn't work; it's been cut off. They'll have to drip dry over the bath. You could hang them on the washing line in the shared yard, I suppose, but…

Lomas

What?

Constance

I wouldn't advise it, that's all. I'll get you the clothes horse.

Lomas

Once I'd hung out my trousers to dry and put the borrowed pair on, she led me through to the lounge. The building couldn't have been more than thirty or forty years old, and yet the interior seemed like that of a much older flat: high ceilings, cracked and flaking; covings painted over so many times they'd gone all lumpy and ill-defined. The faded wallpaper was peeling; the plaster underneath was pitted where fixtures and fittings had come and gone throughout the years. Constance explained that she was planning a bolder colour scheme for the whole room, but it was going to be a big job and she'd only just started yesterday evening. I saw that an inch or two of the dado rail in one corner had gone from drab off-white to translucent smeary pink. On the floor nearby was a bowl of what looked like beetroot juice. Crouching next to it, she dipped in a felt-tip pen and began to dab the liquid onto the rail where the smeary pink left off.

Constance

I've got another pen, if you want to join in. You could start at the opposite end, and we'll meet in the middle.

Lomas

That would probably take several days.

Constance

You think I'm trying to waste your time?

Lomas

No, I'm just saying – it's intricate work. It's clear that very precise strokes of the pen are required. Aside from that, I'm a newcomer to the technique. If I start at the opposite end, I won't have done more than a few millimetres by the time I'm due to leave. No matter how swiftly you work, my side will be dry before you've worked your way across to meet it. There'll be an obvious join, like a tidemark. It won't look good. It won't look professional.

Constance

I see what you mean. That's almost convincing. Yes, I'll take what you say at face value. You can talk to me while I work. What's it like outside?

Lomas

The same as earlier, I think.

Constance

Any sign of spring coming yet?

Lomas

No more so than before.

Constance

Even though I don't go out much these days, I like to know what it's doing, the weather. Back when I still had the radio, it was one of my little pleasures, the shipping and farming news, the forecasts; it gave me a sense of life going on in the outside world, as normal, as it should.

Lomas

Yes, it's useful to know what it's going to do, the weather.

Constance

I used to be really keen on outdoor activities, on the outdoors; that whole outdoor thing, I was always really quite into it. Always hiking up a mountain, that was me, or plunging feet first into a gorge, or rowing a kayak over a lake. I was healthy and active then. Not that I'm unhealthy or inactive now, but I can't afford to get out there as much as I used to; the funds are a problem. Of course the money wasn't exactly brilliant in teaching, but I certainly didn't go short and at least I always had the holidays to look forward to. I tried all sorts of new things. I was always open to challenges.

Lomas

Yes, it's good to try new things. I slept in a forest last night. On a logging track. It was better than some of the disused quarries I've slept in. The car didn't leak, which came as a pleasant surprise, especially since it was raining rather heavily. I kept waking up to check.

Constance

You're slightly obsessive?

Lomas

Not especially. I just kept waking up to check. I couldn't help it.

Constance

Me, I was always slightly obsessive. And highly organized. That's how I found time to cram in as much as I did, the hiking and kayaking, the plunging feet first into gorges, not to mention a busy career. But I had this tendency to break life down into schedules, and the salient characteristic of a schedule is you've always got the end in sight, you're always racing to finish; before you know it, your whole bloody life is one big schedule and you're racing to finish it just like any other kind of schedule – then, at the end of it, there's nothing. Except, you know, death. So what you're doing is, effectively, you're craving your own death. Or at least accelerating your progress towards death. And in my case it was worse, because of this habit I had of taking stock of the past by carving my life up into epochs, which only fore-shortened it, my lifespan as I perceived it, even further. A kind of concertina effect, that's what it was like. So there was the epoch when I lived in a flat by the seaside and listened to light relaxing music, and sometimes went diving at weekends, or sometimes hang-gliding, and did the things I did with a man called Simon, and had a mortgage over a period of ten years, enjoying a favourable fixed rate of interest for the first three. And that was followed by the epoch when I lived in a post-war semi in the suburbs of another town, not by the sea, and listened to early choral music performed in the English cathedral tradition, and did lots of walking at weekends, and did the things I did with Crump, and paid the new mortgage I'd got over twenty-five years at a variable rate for the first three years when the interest rates were low. Each epoch shunted into the next; the defining features of each weren't always all that obvious at the time, but that's how it is, you might not recognize them until afterwards, and by then it's already too late, by then you're stumbling through another part of your life that won't define itself until afterwards, and then once again it's too late. Of course I'm not saying anything clever or original; I had a flat and did a certain thing, and that was the epoch of something or other, and then I had a house and did another thing, and that was the epoch of something else or other, and now I've got no house at all, I'm stuck in this shithole of a flat and don't do anything much, i.e. now it's the epoch of nothing.

Lomas

At least you retain an interest in the weather.

Constance

They say you lose track of time as you get older; you can even lose track of your age. That happened a lot in my early thirties. I'd have to think about it quite hard when someone asked me; I'd have to go back to some memorable event and start counting forwards. But now I'm thirty-nine, I'm all too aware of my age. I don't know how I'll cope with being forty. What about you?

Lomas

I didn't notice. It just slipped by.

Constance

Your fortieth birthday? How could that be?

Lomas

It just slipped by. I wasn't concentrating.

Constance

But you know how old you are now?

Lomas

Yes. I looked into it last Thursday. That's how I know.

Constance

What happened last Thursday?

Lomas

I needed to work out how long it had been since a certain event took place.

Constance

Event?

Lomas

I fell asleep at the top of a cliff. When I woke up, I crawled across the grass at the top of the cliff, to look at the sea below. Some things were floating.

Constance

Can you hear that?

Lomas

What am I listening for?

Constance

That noise. The one next door.

Lomas

I heard a floorboard creaking, and also some muffled voices, but couldn't make out what they were saying. Constance straightened, dropped the pen into the bowl of crimson liquid, and wiped her hands on her chemise. She looked rather panicky.

Constance

You'll find some earplugs in the sideboard. Next to the sleeping tablets. Help yourself to both. Excuse me, please.

Lomas

She rushed from the room. I heard a door slamming shut, a bolt slotting home, the clank of the toilet lid. Because the sanitary dimension of her existence had no bearing on my enquiry, I opened the drawer, selected two earplugs, fresh ones, and put them in as instructed. Then I sat on a stool and waited, listening calmly to the tidal sounds in my head. After twenty minutes, Constance reappeared. She paced up and down for a bit, then gestured for me to take the earplugs out.

Constance

Didn't you take any tablets? I thought you'd be asleep by now.

Lomas

No, I just put these in.

Constance

I thought we could share some. I thought we could sleep until it was over.

Lomas

It didn't bother me all that much. Besides, I wanted to talk about Crump.

Constance

Yes, I mentioned him, didn't I? Earlier.

Lomas

We could go for a drive, if you'd like to get out of the flat.

Constance

So you can fall asleep on a cliff? So you can crawl across the grass to watch me floating in the sea?

Lomas

I thought a picnic site, or a lay-by. There are moors not far from here. Also fields, some woods, and a river. You can see them from the car. Often it looks quite good, the view through a windscreen. Views from windscreens, they can stay with you for years.

Constance

Views more generally, even fleeting ones, not through a windscreen, they can stay with you for years. There's this particular one, for me, with sun and mountains. Before my divorce.

Lomas

With sun and mountains?

Constance

Before my divorce. When I still thought that we were fine, when we weren't fine at all. A road in the mountains, a sweltering road. A weekend away. Girls only, but none of your hen-party carnage, none of your shrieking and squawking while popping out of your bra in the street after midnight, none of your squatting there with your dress hitched up round your hips while everyone watches you making a puddle in the doorway of some exclusive designer boutique. Fresh air and exercise during the day, good food and plenty of wine in the evenings, plenty of talking and laughing and fun. We'd taken the wrong path down from the mountains, but as we trudged back to the hotel I think we all felt we'd had an adventure; we were happy and looking forward to the usual things, a shower, a decent meal and a bottle of wine. And as we trudged along the road I saw these couples, probably also looking forward to their evening, also hot and tired but happy, some holding hands, and then a bottle of wine or whatever, and then a shower, perhaps together, and all that goes with having a shower together, attentively done and mutually considerate. Because that's what you did. A pleasant few days, the sunshine and scenery, food and wine, the various kindnesses in the bedroom or the shower or wherever you chose to do it. I didn't know why I felt so sad, but if I'd looked at it more closely, there and then instead of months later, I might have realized what it meant – that my marriage was over. Because if we'd been one of those couples, tired but happy and trudging back to their hotel rooms hand in hand and into the shower, we would have been different from the rest, we would have ended up embroiled in a series of sticky approximations, it would have been plagiarism, ripping them off, the others and what they were doing.

Lomas

Yes, I've read that it can all be a bit… political.

Constance

When he crawled all over my body, licking and sucking, prising apart new things to explore, pretending they weren't in fact the old things he'd explored in almost exactly the same way a hundred times before, I had the impression that he was rehearsing something he'd seen in a film or read about in a manual, only it wasn't very convincing. Inauthentic – as though he was trying desperately hard to be part of his species, joining in with its anonymous crawl through the darkness and slime of history, but he couldn't quite make it seem natural.

Lomas

Inauthentic, yes. From a manual.

Constance

What if the only thing that set him aside from the rest – the rest of his species – was the fact that he'd stretched a bit further to get his hands on me? Once I started thinking like that, I saw a vast, depersonalized mass of groping and thrusting – not groping hands, not thrusting penises, but groping and thrusting as groping and thrusting and nothing else besides, a kind of cesspit full to the brim of abstract verbs, if cesspits have brims. And what if the physical world, the world of hands and lips and tongues and penises, the world of 'having sex', was just an exercise in form, an imposing of context on an abstract mess in a cesspit where the groping and thrusting and licking and sucking of one human being or body was indistinguishable from the groping and thrusting and licking and sucking of every other body in the world, in human history? So much for his repertoire of tricks; so much for attentively done and mutually considerate.

Lomas

Yes, it's certainly a problem…

Constance

Something had happened to me and I didn't know what it was; I couldn't discuss it, I couldn't begin to, even the words you had to use were a source of revulsion, and not just the verbs, the nouns and adjectives as well. Take 'intimacy', for example: open pores and glistening sebum, breath getting hotter and damper and staler, that whole sense you get of crevices, gussets and moistness. And then there was 'sex life', with its smug implication of near-inevitability – as though everything down there simply took care of itself, or ought to take care of itself, and shouldn't be any more trouble than eating or sleeping. Oddly enough, he didn't mind the term 'sex life' too much; he disliked clichés, but he thought 'sex life' had its uses. That sense of a parallel existence, always present even when hidden, it appealed to him; it was healthy, having a 'sex life' you could drop into when everyday normal life was grinding your face in the dirt, and he used the term frequently when we finally got round to talking about it just before the divorce. Apparently he'd been bored with our sex life for years; he'd always felt that I was *consenting* to it, against my better judgement – not quite grudgingly, but certainly against my better judgement. Consenting to it, with little or no enthusiasm. He conceded that when we got down to it I might seem as though I was enjoying it, and might even attempt within certain rigid boundaries to make it nice for him too, but he always sensed that I was deigning to participate rather than giving myself up to whatever there was, the moment, or the darkness and slime of history, or whatever you give yourself up to. When I asked why he hadn't mentioned this before, he said he'd known it would make me uncomfortable, especially during our dry spells. There was no language up to the task, that's what he claimed; to talk about sex when you aren't having sex and there's no prospect of having sex is so absurd that it just reinforces your celibacy. So the different positions we'd reached, in a way, weren't actually too dissimilar. The divorce was amicable, as far as divorces go.

Lomas

And the man involved – this wasn't Crump?

Constance

No, I was never married to Crump. This was Andrew, who came after. Crump was never one to criticize people like that. He wouldn't have made a woman feel guilty about not doing the things he thought she should have been doing in the bedroom or the shower. He'd suffer in silence if he thought it would spare your feelings.

Lomas

You're quite sure about that?

Constance

Why, you've reason to doubt it?

Lomas

Running away from situations was the one thing he excelled in. What makes you think he'd go on suffering in silence?

Constance

I think you're being a little unfair. Crump was troubled, no denying he was troubled, but he didn't like to burden other people with his problems. Besides, he was hopeless at taking the lead when it came to thrashing things out; he didn't have the people skills. Which was why, incidentally, he never managed to hack it as a teacher: his lack of people skills, his reluctance to impose himself on others, to persuade them to do what he wanted, using people skills.

Lomas

I didn't know about the teaching. There are gaps, you see, in the file.

Constance

That's how we met. He did his training in the department where I worked. He'd come to it later than your average trainee teacher, having tried other things in the meantime that hadn't worked out. Like many idealists, he thought he'd finally found his calling, only he didn't have the temperament. He should really have been a carpenter or a stonemason. Or a fencing master. He could have been a poet, but only a failed one. I always said that in an ideal world he would maybe have been an architect; it would have exercised his creative side in a structured and lucrative way, and would have been more or less achievable as a goal, if only he hadn't lacked the ambition. And the people skills, as I said.

Lomas

It's not a vocation that ever appealed to me. Teaching, I mean.

Constance

I sometimes wonder what would have happened if he'd still been around, still teaching and still working in the same school as me, when I went through the campaign of terror. How he'd have dealt with it, seeing me go through that, and knowing there was nothing he could do.

Lomas

Sorry. I didn't realize about the terror. That you'd been through a campaign of terror.

Constance

Yes – that's why I left the profession. A group of fourteen-year-olds decided it would be amusing to destroy me. They almost succeeded, but not quite. It went on for about six months. I could withstand the threats and abuse, I disregarded the prediction that I'd be abducted at night and buried alive on the wasteground and all that stuff about how they'd release me every so often to be stripped and beaten and dragged around the schoolyard in a gimp mask, I ignored all that and I even fell into line when the deputy head suggested giving it just a bit longer and letting it fizzle out rather than putting the reputation of the school at risk by involving the police, but then this one boy, a real little brute, he tried to assault me one day in class, and when I raised an arm in self-defence, just trying to keep his fist out of my face, you know, deflect it, the bugger cried foul and all the others backed him up, and even the nicer kids felt unable to tell the truth. So I was handcuffed and they escorted me through the school gates with everyone watching, I was put in a marked police car and they took me to the station, where they questioned me at length. And I was suspended, because they always used to suspend you in those cases. And then it got worse. The threats and telephone calls, the public humiliation, stuff through the letterbox… People killed themselves in that kind of situation, people killed themselves, but me, I wasn't about to let the bastards and their shithead parents win. Before the legal proceedings concluded – before they collapsed – I took an administrative job in an office, and did some thinking about what really mattered in life. And I tried to find new meaning in the simple things, in food and drink and friendship and the natural world, and then of course in being together with Andrew, which worked well enough till the business I mentioned earlier. After the divorce, though, when I was vulnerable, things got difficult again. People kept hitting on me – that's what they called it back then, 'hitting on' someone – a stupid phrase, one of many stupid phrases people liked to use for when someone expressed an interest in having sex with someone they weren't having sex with already. Mainly it was men who tried to hit on me, but a couple of women did too. I met this really nice girl through my book club, slightly younger than me, who also liked her walking and the outdoors, we got along well and decided to go for a drink by ourselves one evening, and next thing I knew she was stroking my cheek, and then my neck, which actually felt quite pleasant, though it annoyed me that she'd done it; I'd given no signal to say I was up for being stroked. But like I say, it was the men, unsuitable men, who did it mainly, stroking my cheek without my permission and doing the other things they did when they tried to hit on me, such as looking down my front and calling me Connie. Such a presumption, that, calling me Connie. I thought if I changed my name I might not get so many people hitting on me; I honestly believed that it kept happening because the diminutive of Constance sounds like one of the words for what there is between a woman's legs. By calling me Connie, they were establishing a cheap familiarity, making what was between my legs a degree more accessible, laying it open to further insult and innuendo, in a single word reducing my whole identity to what was between my legs.

Lomas

I take it you didn't.

Constance

What?

Lomas

Change your name.

Constance

No, in the end I came to my senses. I saw that the hitting on me had nothing to do with my name or its diminutive. It had more to do with my job, and the workplace generally. In a conference suite one morning I was confronted by an instruction to give freely of my experience. Something like: 'What you gain from this session will be proportional to what you put into it. Therefore please share our passion for openness and teamwork and give freely of your experience.' I was livid. My experience was my own affair, and taking a militant stand on keeping it private was the only means I had of defending my shrinking place in the world against pricks like these who seemed intent on making life more bloody cretinous by the day. On the floor they had a numbered grid, the kind where each square has room for a hand or foot, some dice are rolled and then the man consults a list. Each group was meant to do their best to stay together in a tangle of limbs and a cloud of morning breath while making their way to the other side of the grid, where a prize awaited. And this was supposed to be fun – the sort of fun that would raise serious points about problem-solving and teamwork. Me, I didn't want to take part, but I was worried about my job – there'd been talk of redundancies – so there I was on my hands and knees, and there was this rancid great arse of a man like a bloody great reeking lobster balancing crossways over my body. One of my ears was in his armpit. He made a remark about my smell. 'Mmm, you smell nice.' I couldn't actually see him leering, but I could hear it in his voice, and I wished him dead. He was more disgusting even than the men who used the diminutive of my name; he was taking a shortcut to the place between my legs and passing comment on what he imagined he'd smell when he got there. But I couldn't say anything to put him down or correct him, because on the face of it he was talking about my perfume, not the place between my legs. Even so, I wished him dead, or better still that he'd never existed, although a peaceful death in his sleep the previous night would have suited me fine. After the exercise, he invited me out for coffee; that's when I realized I'd picked up a loathsome slug who wouldn't leave me alone as long as my movements were a matter of public record – which they were, since my boss was desperate to prove to her boss and everyone else that my daily priorities were consistent with our corporate culture and values. Sure enough, this odious slug began to follow me religiously, sending me cloying little messages, outwardly winsome and light-hearted but always rank with some carnal subtext. It got too much for me again, I decided to look for another job, a job with fewer responsibilities and a lower public profile, but it meant selling up, buying a smaller house in a less desirable area, not to mention a substantial cut in my salary. It also meant I was stuck in an office with a group of women who never stopped talking about sex. Well, that's not true, they talked about other things too – how crap their husbands or boyfriends were, their hatred of certain women in neighbouring offices, and the lack of attention to personal hygiene and grooming among the men, or some of the men, in the neighbouring offices, with particular reference to blackheads, earwax and nasal hair. They were fond of innuendo, these women; their subject, more often than not, was sucking penises, or having their vaginas licked. You bloody well keep your nose to the grindstone as I often say to my Craig, don't talk with your mouth full my Terry's always having to tell me, Brian my Brian he likes to munch on something naughty last thing at night before the lights go out, and talk about appetite me I like my men the way I like my chips, the saltier the better. They were disgusting, but I felt sorry for them in a way; I had the impression that their competitive vulgarity masked an emptiness at the heart of their relationships with other human beings. Listening to them, and seeing how far their existence was shaped by complaint and revulsion, by hatred and disgust for the human body, I couldn't credit them with any kind of sexual generosity. They almost certainly didn't enjoy what they kept talking about; they hated sucking penises, however much they liked to cackle and snort. I couldn't blame them, though, about that part. Myself, I found it revolting, the few occasions I tried it, even though the men I chose to share my life with were always scrupulously clean.

Lomas

So the new job didn't work out.

Constance

No, the new job didn't work out. And despite the smaller house, I couldn't keep up with the mortgage repayments – not by myself, not on that salary. But there was no question of going back to being sniffed and pawed by horrible lecherous slugs, and no question either of going back into the classroom to ward off blows from criminal thugs, so it seemed I was screwed. Incidentally, why are you here? You said you'd help with the redecorating, but you haven't lifted a finger. Why are you here?

Lomas

To find out about Crump.

Constance

That was ages ago. I haven't seen him in years.

Lomas

Something was troubling him.

Constance

Did I say that?

Lomas

You said he was troubled.

Constance

What would you know? Why don't you ask someone else these questions?

Lomas

What questions?

Constance

About his being troubled. About what was troubling him.

Lomas

There's no-one else to ask.

Constance

You could start with Adele.

Lomas

I don't know where she is.

Constance

She lives a few miles from here. I'll take you to her now, if you give me a lift. But we'll have to stop off briefly along the way. I've got an appointment.

Lomas

Her appointment, she explained, was of the medical sort, and not in a good part of town. The bus routes that served the practice were best avoided, as beatings and rapes were all too common, both at the bus stops and on the buses themselves.

Constance

The drivers were told to keep on driving if they heard you being attacked, and because they were scared of repercussions they usually didn't even bother to call it in. Going by taxi wasn't much safer: you might be dragged out and stabbed, or hit round the head with a baseball bat. There was an especially dangerous part where the speed limit dropped to ten miles an hour and they'd take pot shots from the side of the road where the bridge made it easy to hide. I suggested a detour, only Lomas didn't follow my directions and we got lost in a part of town I wasn't familiar with at all. The car smelled funny, a weird sort of chip-shop smell that got right into my clothes.

Lomas

Soon we were travelling through a residential district she was clearly unfamiliar with: small, balconied apartment blocks, cramped, neo-Georgian mews facades, each building set back from the pavement behind its tiny strip of lawn. We'd been driving for almost two hours before she admitted that we were lost.

Constance

When we eventually found our way to a road I recognized, it was too late to be seen at the clinic, so we just drove straight on to Adele's. It was dark by the time we pulled up outside her building, with only a bulb above the main door, a bulb in a cage, to light our way between the heaps of scrap in the yard. I snagged my chemise a couple of times, and in the loading bay, where they'd laid on emergency lighting, I could see that my pashmina was ripped in two places, which annoyed me.

Lomas

The corridor smelled of uncollected refuse and blocked drains, the air was colder than outside, and there was a stairway, dimly lit, which we ascended. Several storeys up, we found ourselves on a landing with no means of climbing further. Constance hesitated, saying she'd thought there were two more floors; Adele lived one floor from the top, so maybe we needed to go back down a floor. From the landing below we gained access to a passageway lined with small doors. I was about to say that maybe we'd got the wrong building, that this was clearly a disused factory and not an apartment block, when Constance made a triumphant noise and directed me to a door on the left-hand side.

Constance

What gave it away was the fact that one of the doors was scratched around the keyhole, so it must have been Adele's, because of her terrible spatial awareness. Really clumsy, she was.

I knocked but there was no answer, so I opened the door and felt around for a switch. The light bulb worked, and there was a mattress in the centre of the floor, and also a stool, which I took while Lomas stood by the window.

Lomas

We'd been waiting for half an hour, saying nothing, when the bulb went out. The light from the corridor wasn't enough to make much difference, and Constance was uneasy with the idea of sitting waiting with the main door open, so I edged round to the two interior doors. My hands passed over metal and ceramics – I guessed that one cupboard had been converted into a washroom and the other into a walk-in kitchenette – but I found no light switch. As I was groping around and patting, Constance called out.

Constance

Just to warn you, right: I've moved onto the mattress. I'm really cold.

Lomas

I'll stay over here, then.

Constance

There's no quilt on the bed. There isn't even a sheet.

Lomas

Shall I find you a towel to use instead?

Constance

No. Adele might be offended if you start going through her things. Besides, the towels are bound to be damp.

Lomas

Do you want to use my coat?

Constance

Then you'll be cold too. Adele used to work long shifts; we could be here till morning. You'll get pneumonia or something.

Lomas

I'll drive you home, if you like.

Constance

Too dangerous, this time of night. No, we'll just have to make the best of it. I get the impression that you're a gentleman who won't try anything funny if we huddle together for warmth. You can curl up against my back and put your coat over the two of us. That'll be fine.

Lomas

I did as she advised, suppressing a mild surge of anxiety for my box file, which I'd left in the boot of the car.

4

Lomas

I very much needed to sleep, but sleep wouldn't come. Although I tried to empty my mind of troublesome thoughts and associations, I was distracted by the harsh synthetic texture of Constance's garments, and even more so by the rigidity of her posture, which contrasted strangely with the rhythm of her breathing – steady and slow, the breathing of someone who was already in deep sleep. When I did nod off, the sleep I got was fitful, and when I woke up it was to the conviction that something had changed about the person lying next to me. While we'd been arranging ourselves, I'd noticed that her hair smelled slightly vinegary – not offensively so, but sharply enough to cut through my own stale smell. Now it smelled biscuity, not vinegary. In addition, she felt easier to feel, in a way I couldn't fully define. One obvious factor was her main garment, which felt like cotton, although there was more to it than the merits of natural fibres over synthetic ones. While I was reflecting on this, she changed position, displacing my hand from her side; I couldn't see her, but I sensed that she was staring at me. When she spoke, her voice wasn't Constance's voice. It wasn't Saoirse's either; nor was it Juniper's. Perhaps, I thought, the voice belonged to Adele. But apart from the voice, the lack of a vinegary smell, the texture of the chemise or other main garment, and the way that she felt easier to feel, the person lying on the mattress seemed exactly like the person I'd lain down with some hours earlier in an attempt to conserve our warmth.

Adele

Are you the landlord?

Lomas

No. Do I look like the landlord?

Adele

You might do. It's been a while since I last saw him. Besides, I can't see you.

Lomas

I can assure you I'm not the landlord. Property ownership isn't my strong point. I've got no portfolio.

Adele

Did my mother send you?

Lomas

No. I've never met your mother, as far as I'm aware.

Adele

I'm pleased to hear it.

Lomas

I could see that if I risked calling her Adele and she proved not to be, my behaviour would seem gauche to the point of boorishness – especially when, in a sense, we'd spent the night together, albeit only some of the night, a couple of hours, and spent them chastely at that. At any rate, I decided that a degree of circumspection would be advisable in my questioning. So I asked her why she'd asked me what she'd asked, about being the landlord.

Adele

Did I say you were the landlord?

Lomas

Not exactly. You just asked.

Adele

I was probably still half-asleep. You know, half-dreaming.

Lomas

Yes, I see.

Adele

Even so, you could be acting on his behalf. A kind of emissary or envoy.

Lomas

Like a bailiff?

Adele

Not quite that.

Lomas

You don't hold the bailiff in high regard as a professional class?

Adele

I've no experience of the class. I've never entered into any form of credit agreement. I've never even fallen behind with the rent.

Lomas

Does the landlord normally get into bed with you when he comes to collect the rent?

Adele

Did you get into bed with me? Or did I get into bed with you?

Lomas

I don't remember.

Adele

The owner of this place, he never comes round. That's how I like it. In the other place it was different. There was a landlord and a landlady. They were horrible. Always coming round and intruding. I actually hated them.

Lomas

They both got into bed with you?

Adele

Not exactly. That would have been awful.

Lomas

Yes, it would have been. If you hated them.

Adele

She was the nastier of the two. He just stared at me and probed his gums with his tongue. He was disgusting, but she was worse.

Lomas

What did she do?

Adele

She was a bully. In a way that would have been difficult to prove, if there'd been anyone to prove it to. Which there wasn't.

Lomas

I see what you mean.

Adele

You do?

Lomas

Well… renting, it can be a bit of a lottery.

Adele

They had cameras in the flat. Hidden cameras, recording

everything I did. Even in the bathroom.

Lomas

You had proof of that?

Adele

Like I said before, I didn't have any proof. I just suspected it. I imagined them laughing and pointing at the pictures, and showing the pictures to their friends, and putting them up for the rest of the world to see, if the rest of the world wanted to look.

Lomas

You didn't investigate?

Adele

No, because finding out and seeing it would have been worse. Naively, I confided in my mother.

Lomas

This is the person you were glad I hadn't met.

Adele

Yes, that's the one. I wouldn't have bothered, except she kept on saying she wanted us to be close again, like before – like we had been when I was younger, so she said. And because she kept on saying it, over and over, I kind of gave in from time to time, and let her get closer than I should have. By confiding.

Lomas

Those sorts of family situations can be tricky, so I've heard.

Adele

I always said that if they let themselves into the flat while I was in bed and they started peering under the covers, pushing their cameras in for a close-up, then I'd terminate my tenancy agreement and move away without leaving a forwarding address. As it happened, things came to a head when I had the problem with the shower.

Lomas

I'm not keen on them myself. Reliability. Me, I'd sooner take a bath.

Adele

Well yes, I'd tried that, but it wasn't really much better. Whenever I turned on the taps, these lumps of snotty black sludge came out; it wasn't very nice. I'd tried boiling water up in the kitchen, too, in pans, and taking the pans through into the bathroom and doing it that way, but it was taking far too long to fill the tub. I had no option but to phone them and say look, there's no hot water coming out of the shower. What I remember most about crowding into the bathroom with the two of them was the smell. I used to spend hours scrubbing away with disinfectants, bleaches, grouting cleaners, you name it, antibacterial sprays, but it always stank of mould, the bathroom, always, and now I could smell her horrible perfume as well, and her breath, and her husband's underclothes, not to mention his lunchtime alcohol and the ketones from the fried breakfasts he ate twice a day. Even before I started explaining the problem, my chest felt so tight I almost couldn't breathe, and I could see from their expressions that they believed – or they wanted me to believe – that I was making the whole thing up. And so the words just stuck in my throat. She told me to tell her and not to be shy, and when I said about the hot water, she told me to demonstrate. It was awkward because they'd hemmed me in and I didn't want to get closer to them than I was, but if I'd switched it on, the shower, with them standing right next to the bath, they would have been drenched in freezing cold water. She got impatient then, and told me to stand in the bath while her husband waited outside on the landing. I took my slippers off, and my socks, and got in and drew the curtain in front of me, leaving a gap so I could see. When she said about switching it on, I made some apologetic remark about the water, how I'd get wet, and she said what of it, isn't getting wet the whole point of taking a shower, and I said no, I meant my clothes, my clothes will get wet, and she said what, are you trying to tell me you keep your clothes on in the shower? By now I felt quite intimidated, but I told myself at least her husband was still outside the bathroom, and as long as he stayed outside then nothing would happen. I suppose that's why I gave in. I took off my jumper and T-shirt and rolled them up and put them on the windowsill. When I tried to undo my belt and unzip my jeans, I had to force my fingers to work, my hands were like claws, but somehow I got them off, my jeans, and folded them up – and then I just stood there, hunched and shivering, in my underwear. Mrs Alderson was glaring at me in a way that seemed to imply I was wasting her time, and then she looked pointedly at the parts of me still covered. I shook my head. She said she'd brought up three girls, three beautiful girls of her own, and not to kid myself – whatever I had was nothing special at all, and who the hell did I think I was, she'd seen it a thousand times before. To stop the insults more than anything else – this stupid, crass way she was talking – I added my bra to the pile. But that was it; I refused to take my knickers off. Absolutely. I just refused. And she must have realized I wouldn't be swayed, because eventually she sighed and pulled the curtain across and said switch on the shower. When the water came out, I stepped back out of the way, and she reached in and turned the dial right up and said did it make any difference. I could tell that it was freezing, and I said so, but she wasn't happy with that and said put your head under the water. Apparently that was the only way to find out, I'd have to pretend I was washing my hair, so I edged forwards, trying to cover myself by crossing my arms on my front, but once my head was under the water it was so bad I had to raise both hands to shield my head from the cold. How long I stayed under, I don't know; it seemed like ages, though it was probably just a few seconds. When I backed out, the curtain was open and Mr Alderson was standing in the bathroom. He was staring at my tits, and he had this look on his face, this critical expression, as though they hadn't quite lived up to his expectations. I stared back – a doomed attempt to project a vestige of defiance through all the shame and mortification, I suppose – but he just probed his gums with his tongue and turned his attention to my knickers, which were soaked and not concealing the details that knickers, sensible knickers, are meant to conceal. Mrs Alderson gave me a towel. 'We'll have to get in touch with the plumber,' she said. 'He'll contact you direct. Don't trouble to see us out. And make sure you've got some clothes on when the plumber comes round. He'll think you're a right little slut. The electrician was just saying, last time we saw him, wasn't he, Jack? She's a filthy, prick-teasing whore, that's what he said. We'll be in touch about the rent. We're due for a rise, if I remember. See you later, Adele.' I stood there with the towel until I heard them slam the door. I put my bathrobe on and crouched down by the windowsill and peered until I saw them drive away. And then I locked all the doors and windows and closed all the curtains and put the heating on and dried my hair with the dryer on full blast and then I went to bed and stayed there for three days.

Lomas

Without interruption?

Adele

No, I got up to go to the toilet. And towards midnight of the second day, I made it as far as the kitchen so I could eat a square of dark chocolate and drink some brandy. Quite a lot of brandy, actually. Half a bottle. I wasn't used to drinking that much, but it was useful, it induced a strange lucidity. Back in bed, I glimpsed the truth of my situation. I was so weak I couldn't even keep my clothes on when my fifty-five-year-old landlady, a parvenu I didn't even respect, gave the order to strip. And then there was

the fear that it was going to be a matter of public record, because
of the cameras. When I imagined how the footage of my pathetic,
cringing body would be received in the wider world, I didn't see
how it would be possible to go on living. If Renton Curtis happened to see it, I'd be finished.

Lomas

Renton Curtis?

Adele

Just this wanker who'd made it his business to get too close to
me, years before. He was a patient at the hospital where I was
treated after the failure of my career. Well, I say patient; he was
really just one of those fashionable lifestyle depressives who managed to get themselves on telly from time to time. Preposter-
ously, he saw himself as my mentor – or me as his muse. He was
a charlatan, a fraud with unpleasant behavioural problems, a
creep who exploited the trendy idea of mutual support as a means
of opening up financial opportunities – also sexual ones, if he
could. I can't remember the name of the memoir he got published about his fight against mental illness, but it was lauded on
daytime TV, and they invited him on a couple of times to plug it,
both before and after the trial.

Lomas

The trial?

Adele

For tax evasion. My mother really liked him, or at least she didn't
see him as a threat. He'd known my sister-in-law at school;
they'd been quite friendly, and he played on the connection.
Soon he was practically a member of the family.

Lomas

You asked if I was the landlord. Then you asked if your mother had sent me. You didn't ask if I'd been sent by Renton Curtis.

Adele

Renton wouldn't have sent someone. Renton would have come himself, if he'd known. If you'd been Renton, you'd have been whispering things: reproaches for not writing, for shutting you out. You'd have been trying to make me feel guilty even before I'd woken up.

Lomas

Why the question about your mother?

Adele

Because she's been trying to persuade me to return. From time to time she sends out people to entice me, people with babies, only she hasn't been able to find me, not for a while. That's the advantage of living your life in a dump like this, and that's why she's always disapproved of it, the way I keep moving around and not telling anyone where I'm going. I should settle down and have children instead, apparently, and the fact that I won't is the source of all my problems. So when the Aldersons were after me, she blamed me for it, what she believed of it, saying if only I'd taken control of my life and settled down with some decent bloke with decent sperm and decent DIY skills, it wouldn't be happening – if it was happening, which she didn't believe it was. And when Renton was harassing me, it was all in my head, and Renton could have been good for me if only I'd had the sense to give him a chance. That was before the tax bust. It was her solution to everything, settling down and having babies, as though having a husband and children would stop me from being a target. If you weren't so unsettled and skittish, making a show of yourself, you wouldn't attract such nutters all the time, that's what she said. And when it got really bad with Renton, when he was standing outside my flat all night and staring up at the window, I panicked and phoned her and asked for help, and her solution was to smuggle me out to the holiday home, the brood farm where my sisters and some of my sisters-in-law and their friends were staying together.

Lomas

That must have been grim.

Adele

All these children, screaming and fighting and pissing and shitting, while the mothers waddled from sofa to fridge and back again with their arse-cracks showing, all gorging themselves on cake and Australian chardonnay and cooing about how cute it was, the screaming and pissing and shitting. Actually, the children weren't too bad; it was the mothers who really disgusted me. They talked about lactating together, and cooking and eating placentas. They assumed the only reason I hadn't dragged a brood of my own along was my terrible luck with men. One of them even took me aside to recommend an ex-boyfriend who'd be willing to act as a sperm donor. 'It'll be great,' she said, 'he's a lovely bloke, and once you're on your way I could maybe show you how to express yourself.' It took me a moment to realize she didn't mean scaling the heights of creative endeavour; she was talking about the art of squeezing milk out from my tits. Then there was her friend, who explained how her son was rejecting the teat now that she'd stopped eating chocolate caramels; chocolate milkshake had been coming out of her tits, the kid had got used to it, he'd got fussy and now he wouldn't drink anything else. I had to get out of there but I couldn't just announce that I was going; it would have looked odd, like I was a moody bitch who hated mothers and children. So I packed my bag and sneaked out early next morning without saying anything. Of course when my absence was discovered, they thought that anyway: I was a moody bitch who hated mothers and children. My mother was furious. 'They were trying to help you,' she said, 'they were trying to make you feel safe.' I pointed out that if she'd wanted me to feel safe she wouldn't have sent me to stay with Renton's old friend Carla, my pregnant sister-in-law, but as usual the discussion ended up being about my failure to produce children. 'It's not as if you need to keep your voice intact; the singing's no excuse, you're not even trying any more.' I'd always used my classical singing career as a justification for childlessness, you see; I'd told my mother that singers are rarely as good after childbirth. Something breaks inside the body. All that pushing and straining and bellowing – the voice can lose a lot of its sweetness of tone, and it seems to be worse if you're a soprano. My mother claimed that a woman who didn't have children could never be truly and fully a woman. But she also valued material success and she thought that a woman should have a lucrative career. She could countenance, just about, my not being truly and fully a woman as long as it seemed I might be successful. But then the success thing passed me by. 'If you're not going to have a career and you're not going to settle down and have children, what are you going to do with your life?' Well, I didn't know what I was going to do with my life, so that's where the conversation ended. All I wanted was to fade into the background, to be less present and less tangible. I wanted to live in absolute silence.

Lomas

Sorry. I shouldn't have kept you talking. By the way, what happened to Constance?

Adele

Oh, she had to go back to her flat. Something to do with her redecorating project. Would you mind if I went to sleep for a while? We can talk when I next wake up. You can put your hand on my waist if you want. Like before.

Lomas

I did as she said, and slept quite well, and woke at dawn to find myself alone in the room. Peering through the window, I saw a woman moving swiftly between the heaps of rubble and scrap in the yard below. It looked like Constance, though it was difficult to be sure. I put on my coat and went straight down, but after half an hour of driving round the area, failing to spot her or anyone like her, I gave up. There was a public toilet across the road from where I stopped the car, so I got my toothbrush and soap and performed some basic ablutions. As I was drying my face, my phone made a curious noise. Perhaps it had switched itself on in the night, while we'd been using my coat as a blanket; I hadn't been able to pick up a signal or even gain access to a function menu for weeks, but now it seemed fine. I had a message from Bettina, dated almost three months earlier.

Bettina

Can you call in? There's something we need to discuss. Quite urgent, but don't worry. Do take care.

Lomas

Calling in, as she put it, was going to prove rather difficult, as my fuel was getting low and I had no idea where the next slug of vegetable oil would be coming from. I felt I should be looking more closely at Constance and Adele, at how I'd conflated their identities – if I'd conflated their identities – and so, with that in mind, I headed for Constance's flat. She still had my trousers. They should be dry by now, and I'd soon have further need of them.

5

Lomas

Again she was dressed in the brown-and-orange housecoat, which had been washed and carefully mended since the incident with the truck. Standing in the doorway, she stared at me vacantly for a long moment. I kept expecting her to ask me who I was and what I wanted, but she said nothing. I thought about mentioning the way she'd disappeared, and was she all right, and had Adele been telling the truth about the redecorating, but somehow it seemed inappropriate. Who was I to demand that Constance account for her movements?

Constance

I'd forgotten to cover the bowl, the bowl with the stain in for the dado rail, and I thought it might evaporate or something. It just sort of came to me in the middle of the night, and once it was there it got stuck in my brain and kept going round and round and it stopped me, really, from sleeping. Really vexing, it was. So I went.

Lomas

In the end I just told her I'd come for my trousers. It was the truth.

Constance

I needn't have worried, in fact. My wood stain hadn't dried up. And Lomas hadn't come to tell lies about wanting to help out with the project; he'd just come for his trousers. I couldn't remember what I'd done with them, so I went and checked the obvious places, the bathroom and the bedroom and the airing cupboard, and when I got back to the lounge I found him looking rather shifty.

Lomas

She'd made some progress with the dado rail, about six inches of which had now been stained with beetroot juice or whatever she was using.

Constance

When I say shifty, I mean I got the strong impression that he'd been listening in on the neighbours.

Lomas

It took her an hour to find my trousers and hand them over. They felt stiff and somehow strange. I wondered whether she'd given me someone else's in error, but quickly dismissed the idea; the trousers were mine. My old green corduroys. I folded them. She gestured at the wall.

Constance

That's the problem with working on that side of the room. You get distracted. Your head's too close to the wall, and you hear it, stuff that's going on next door.

Lomas

I didn't hear anything. But my head wasn't close to the wall. I wasn't on that side of the room.

Constance

She's got people in. You can hear them, but you can't tell what they're doing, not exactly. You have to interpret the creaks and voices as best you can. The voices are muffled, so it's hard to draw conclusions.

Lomas

At least you've managed another few inches.

Constance

I could get you a glass if you wanted. A tumbler or beaker. It's good for amplifying sound, they say – like a stethoscope.

Lomas

Me, I'm just as happy not knowing.

Constance

To be honest, she seems decent enough in herself; it's the people who visit who cause all the problems, if you can categorize them as problems. I know you shouldn't rush to judge, I know you shouldn't draw moral conclusions, and I daresay if I knew what was going on – if I was in full possession of the facts, instead of just bits and pieces drifting through the wall – then I'd be assured that it was all innocent, perfectly innocent. That's why I could do with having a stethoscope.

Lomas

Perhaps you could get one from the clinic.

Constance

I'm going there later.

Lomas

May I offer you a lift?

Constance

To the clinic? That's kind.

Lomas

You'll have to direct me. Have you got a decent road map?

Constance

I'm afraid not.

Lomas

I was probably wrong about the stethoscope.

Constance

Yes, they don't give those things out.

Lomas

But you could buy one somewhere, surely.

Constance

True. The problem is, it escalates. You sometimes get fixated. Like I said earlier, you shouldn't rush to criticize. You never know how bad you might sound yourself. Only last week, for example, I got up in the middle of the night and accidentally slammed a door. It must have sounded terrible to anyone who heard.

Lomas

Crump, too, was sensitive to noise, from what I've been told.

Constance

Crump was sensitive to lots of things. Pretty much everything was a potential source of anxiety.

Lomas

Such as bad weather?

Constance

No, not bad weather, but plenty of other things. Being out in a storm was something Crump found bracing; he climbed mountains in the winter and had no problem with being lashed by wind and rain. What made him anxious were banal things – trivial, localized things, like noises in the street, what might be going on down the street, and whether we'd leave the house next morning to find the wipers of my car bent back or scratches along the side.

The threats were trivial in themselves, but the effect was cumulative; there was a sense of impending disaster that got so pervasive it seemed to render him incapable of normal human relations – until in the end he could barely bring himself to touch me. I remember once we were packing our bags for a couple of days away – this was when we were trying to find enjoyable things to do, to calm him down and make life seem a little less threatening than it had done, more benign, like when we first met – and I noticed him carefully packing some condoms, as though he genuinely believed that we'd be getting up to all the tricks that other couples got up to, or were supposed to get up to, on long weekends away. Seeing him preparing for something that wasn't going to happen because he was no longer capable of making it happen was touching and really quite sad; he reminded me of a self-contained little boy who was packing a knapsack for a nature walk or a trip to the zoo or something, only whatever it was, despite his preparations and the reading on the topic he'd done in advance, it was going to disappoint him somehow, or possibly not even happen at all. But going away for nice weekends, or what were meant to be nice weekends, that wasn't the only thing we tried when we were looking for ways to stop his anxiety from ruining his life, and ruining mine by association. I showed him some yoga – just the basics, but enough to take his mind off things for a while. He didn't stick at it, though. Drinking too much was easier, so he drank too much instead. And then he became obsessed with getting rid of his belongings. He threw a heap of stuff away.

Lomas

Yes, I've heard a lot, admittedly none of it very precise, about his early political views. Was throwing away his belongings a reaffirmation of what he believed when he was younger?

Constance

There was nothing political about it, as far as I'm aware. He decided that the origins of his fear lay in the ownership of material things – or, to be more precise, in the shared investment of two people in domestic private property. As he saw it, an attack on the house or the car would be an attack on our life together, or on me, which wasn't a prospect he could live with. Perhaps I made it worse, because I was always quite attached to material things. If I lost a glove, or smashed a favourite mug in the kitchen, I'd get upset – sometimes to the point of tears. Although he didn't have a share in the house, he helped to pay the mortgage while we were living together. This counted, in his view, as a form of mutual investment, so it followed that we'd already made ourselves an easy target for violation by the mob. Throwing out all his gear, or giving it to charity shops or whatever, was just the beginning of his peculiar counter-initiative.

Lomas

Couldn't he have sold it and spent the proceeds on more drink?

Constance

He didn't own the sort of stuff that would turn a profit. So he just binned it, or gave it to charity shops or whatever. Soon he was talking about moving out. It would be better for our relation-ship, he claimed – as if hardly seeing each other would bring us closer together. I asked him where he planned to live and how he expected to pay the rent, especially when he'd dropped out of teaching by then and was getting by on a series of low-paid dead-end jobs. I never really got a coherent answer to that, but he sometimes mentioned Anderson shelters, shepherds' bothies, bivouacs and tents. That was probably the main reason for our relationship ending: the fact that he'd rather sleep rough than share a house with me. When he left, it was all very amicable, no bitterness or anything, just a sadness on both sides, and a feeling on my part that I could have done more to help him. Not long afterwards, though, I heard that he was living with somebody else. It left me nonplussed, I have to admit. Did he feel less pro-tective towards this new woman than towards me? Was he simply

using her, using her flat as a place to sleep in, a sort of bolthole
he could abandon at short notice? Had he been lying all along
about the fear because he couldn't see me as a viable long-term
partner in a long-term domestic investment? Or had being with
me sapped his confidence so much that it was impossible for him
to enjoy a normal life surrounded by nice things?

Lomas

I see your point.

Constance

So you say. You've no idea what it was like.

Lomas

You're right, I haven't.

Constance

Why are you asking me these questions?

Lomas

I'm starting to wonder.

Constance

So now I'm boring you? You think you can insult me?

Lomas

It was an accident. My attention wandered. I'm sorry.

Constance

What right have you to interrogate me, anyway?

Lomas

None whatsoever.

Constance

So why are you doing this?

Lomas

I called round to pick up my trousers.

Constance

Don't be evasive. I mean these questions of yours about Crump.

Lomas

Well, I'd say he's got some explaining to do, wouldn't you? That's all. I think he needs to justify himself.

Constance

For all his questions, Lomas was no help when it came to explaining why Crump had shunned our domestic arrangement. He just made some bland, bureaucratic remark about how there was nothing in his box file, as far as he knew, that cast any light on the matter I'd raised.

Lomas

What I said about him having some explaining to do and maybe needing to justify himself was simply an off-the-cuff remark, and yet as soon as I'd spoken I realized that this mildly pompous indictment was in fact a more or less accurate representation of my attitude to Crump. The realization was especially significant as I hadn't been aware until this point that I actually had a particular attitude to Crump. The man had been the subject of an enquiry; my view of him had been neutral, utterly neutral, by default. Now I'd erred towards disapproval, and felt compelled to ask how creditable my disapproval was. How far was it conditioned, for example, by an urge to ingratiate myself with the people he'd left behind – the people I could all too easily classify as his victims? And why did I see them as victims? Was there a salacious or predatory motive? Knowing what I knew about myself, I felt that such a theory could be summarily dismissed, but there remained the possibility that I was drawn to that which was wretched, defeated and hopeless about these women. Perhaps I was little more than a grief whore. It wasn't an edifying thought, but then again it wasn't conclusive. All I could conclude with any authority was that I no longer subscribed to the assumption which had underpinned my enquiry from the beginning, namely that Crump had gained certain insights into the nature of human existence and so forth. If he had really gained such insights – which he'd been ill-equipped to do, if the anecdotal evidence were to be believed – he had manifestly failed to pass on the benefits of those insights to these unfortunate former acquaintances of his, whose lives, it seemed to me, he'd played a substantial part in ruining. And I decided that from now on I should refer to these former acquaintances not as 'victims' but as 'attestants'. It seemed better from a moral point of view.

All this undoubtedly put my enquiry in a new light, but it also raised a major procedural dilemma. If I continued to frame the project in terms of the issue of Crump's disappearance and putative insights, I'd be lending credibility – superficially at least – to the idea that what he'd done entailed some broader human significance. I didn't believe in revelations or epiphanies; any insights he'd gained were probably variations on the obvious truth that running away from awkward situations could provide a fleeting sense of release. It was clear that if the enquiry were to continue, what would sustain my dwindling interest would not be Crump but the attestants – to whom, however, Crump and his story remained my only really convincing means of access. In short, I'd have to go on pretending I still cared about his doings, whatever they were.

Constance

It kind of jarred a bit, to be honest, the way he'd made the link with Crump when we'd been talking about the noises from next door. Suddenly it all became about Crump, and he wouldn't say why. I found it intrusive and quite strange.

Lomas

She hadn't replied to the glib remark I'd made about Crump. She was just staring at the front window, which had been covered in sheets of old newspaper, stuck down with tape. I mentioned Adele then, how we'd talked on my last visit about how Constance knew where she lived and might be able to take me to see her.

Constance

Adele?

Lomas

That's right. You told me she lived not far from here.

Constance

I've got a medical appointment, I'm afraid.

Lomas

Don't worry, I'll take you. And then the three of us, we could sit down together for tea. Assuming she's got some. If she hasn't, we could buy some on the way.

Constance

She won't have a kettle. Or it's unlikely she will. I haven't got one either. Not one that works.

Lomas

We'll get you a new one.

Constance

We?

Lomas

You've helped me out with my trousers. So I'd be happy to pay, to meet the cost of a kettle, in return. If that's all right, I mean. I wouldn't want you to take the suggestion amiss.

Constance

I prefer to pay my own way. Gifts from strangers make me uneasy, for obvious reasons. Anyway, where do you expect to find a kettle for sale around here?

Lomas

A second-hand hardware shop, perhaps.

Constance

It wouldn't be new. It'd be second-hand, not new.

Lomas

But some of these old kettles, pre-electrics, they're almost antiques. They don't even have to be made of copper. Even battered old aluminium ones with black handles can boast an unpretentious charm.

Constance

It's just… It all seems rather hopeless.

Lomas

But you'll come? I mean, you'll join us?

Constance

Why would I want to?

Lomas

Well, the discussion might be productive. And if she's got tea —

Constance

What makes you think I'm so bloody interested in tea? Let's just go.

Lomas

When we set off, with Constance navigating, it felt as though we were travelling in the wrong direction, or certainly the opposite one from last time. I said nothing for a while, just kept on driving; she directed me onto a dual carriageway leading out of town, and in the absence of further instructions I assumed that continuing straight ahead was what I was meant to do. When I did look over, to check that my assumption was correct, I saw that she'd fallen asleep, and her mouth was hanging open. Catching flies, they used to call it. I pulled over into a lay-by, partly to wait for her to wake up and get her bearings, and partly to watch her with her mouth open, catching flies. The open mouth in sleep, I recalled, had always been associated, disproportionately so, with the elderly sleeper, and this filled me with a crushing sense of pity, both for the elderly in general and more particularly for Constance, whose mouth had already become an old woman's mouth and was so consummately an old woman's mouth that its influence had spread across the rest of her face, which accordingly was now an old woman's face, although her hair remained unaffected. I wondered whether her body, slumped and inscrutable in the boiler suit she'd chosen for the journey, had been transformed into an elderly woman's body, and then I felt guilty. And then I felt nothing. Because it must happen all the time, this transform-ation, or one just like it; it must happen to all sorts of people, in cars, on trains; watching it was something you couldn't avoid. When she woke up, she would revert to her younger self again; her mouth would close, her mouth would cease to catch flies, but her body would still be a vulnerable composite of tissues, fluids and hairs, a vulnerable composite that would soon begin to go wrong, to fail, to disintegrate irrevocably, as composites do, both singly and in pairs, as I remembered, though the details of how the process worked in pairs was rather hazy. There was love, of course, and necessity, yes, and the will to survive, yes, naturally – but how did the illusion work, what exactly were the mechanics of overlooking and forgetting? Something to do with *not* overlooking or forgetting – that was the point; there was that paradox you weren't supposed to think about, not too deeply, not if you wanted it to continue. I tried to identify a more general manifestation of the paradox, one in which human sensibility wasn't a factor, but all I could come up with was an image of two birds, one male, one female, blinking in mechanical bewilderment from a nest. It was as close as I could get to reflective commentary on the problem. Meanwhile Constance was still sleeping with her mouth open, and again, as during the incident in the toilet, I had the feeling that some basic human response was required, only this time it was required to impose some meaning on the spectacle of her open mouth, and also to redeem my tasteless lapse into an unhelpful way of thinking.

Constance

I'd fallen asleep. When I woke up, he'd driven miles and miles out of town, but then he'd realized and done a U-turn at a roundabout and gone back.

Lomas

And soon enough Constance was awake, a younger woman again, not an elderly one. She stretched and looked around. After a minute or two she directed me down a side street.

Constance

Mount the kerb in front of the warehouse.

Lomas

Is that where she lives?

Constance

No, her building's just round the corner. But there aren't enough places to park in, and the competition for spaces leads to disputes. Someone got killed the other week – stabbed, for taking someone else's place, or what someone liked to think of as his place. There was this argument, and he died from multiple stab wounds. What are you doing?

Lomas

I'd been dithering, wondering what to do with the box file, undecided whether to bundle it under my coat or leave it locked up in the boot, and I was still fumbling with it, trying to fasten my buttons over the top, when Constance arrived at a narrow crossroads up ahead. She made an elaborate, two-handed gesture towards an entrance between two high walls topped with razor wire, then waved goodbye and turned the corner opposite.

Constance

I'd had enough of messing about. And I was late for my appointment. So I thought it best we went our separate ways.

Lomas

And then this figure appeared from further up the road. She was hurrying, staying as close as she could to the wall; it was clear that she was trying to blend in subtly with her surroundings, but in doing so she was making herself conspicuous in a way that put her at risk of being singled out and picked on. In one hand she carried a broad-brimmed polythene bowl. As she darted into the entrance that Constance had indicated, a group of children emerged from the corner opposite, jostling Constance in their midst. They were jabbing her belly and buttocks with what looked like hunting crops, and squirting her with liquid – I assumed it was underage urine – from toy pistols. I felt a compulsion to intervene, but feral children lay beyond my expertise; they wouldn't be swayed by a creaky old sod with rotten shoes

and a faltering voice, and it would be Constance who'd be pun-
ished for my inadequacies. And Constance herself, from what I
could see, was of the same mind. Rolling her eyes and emitting
muffled exclamations, she was waving me away; I had the impression that this encounter had taken place several times before,
and that she was embarrassed to think that her part in it might be
observed by a relative stranger. Meanwhile the woman with the
polythene bowl was about to be lost among piles of rubbish
further down the lane. Setting off after her, I risked a quick glance
back at Constance, who was struggling with two of the children
as they tried to unzip her boiler suit at the front.

Crump [box file]

Some stupid piece of horseplay, it was. Bizarrely uncharacter-
istic, and on my part wholly regrettable. It was something
couples did; I don't know why. Some doubtless thought of it as
play-fighting; if it wasn't actually play-fighting, they thought of it
as fun. It wasn't fun. Her jaw was set, and she was frowning –
like a small girl trying to wrest a favourite toy back from an older
child, a stronger child, the sneering bully who'd seized it. There
was that hopeless determination; innocent stubbornness with the
knowledge of inalienable right on its side. I took it away with me,
that image; it had a photographic clarity. Overlaying it, however,
was a coterminous distortion, a corrupted variation, showing an
open mouth with a straining black tongue and two rows of
stumps where her teeth had crumbled, the whole face frozen
horribly in mid-howl […] as if I needed to be reminded […] the
accretions of human dignity […] stripped […] an instant […] the
unalloyed self […] revealed […] no different […] any other […]
self […]

Lomas

Soon I was trespassing, ducking through holes in wire fences,
stealing through yards filled with broken masonry and scrap
metal, keeping the woman in sight, the polythene bowl in sight,

until I finally came to a room in a derelict warehouse where a radiator was spurting dirty water from a hairline crack in its base. The woman was using the bowl to collect the water; when it was full to the brim, she stanched the flow with her thumb and glanced rather desperately at the Belfast sink on the other side of the room. After a minute or so, she rushed across and emptied it, leaving the radiator free to spurt more water onto the floor. She was back down by the radiator and contemplating a second dash to the sink before she noticed me in the doorway.

Adele

Hello. Are you any good at plumbing?

Lomas

I'm afraid not.

Adele

Oh, that's a blow. I thought you might be able to help.

Lomas

I suppose we could try to shut off the taps. Have you got an adjustable spanner?

Adele

I haven't got any kind of spanner.

Lomas

If you had, we might have been able to shut off the taps. It might have given you some breathing space, some time to mop up the gunk and bring in a plumber. Except I've just noticed that your radiator has a thermostatic valve. Shutting the taps off wouldn't have worked – even with an adjustable spanner. With a thermostatic valve, you think you're shutting that side off by turning the dial right down to zero, but the water, it just keeps on coming through, even if you've closed the system down at the opposite end.

Adele

Yes, I did try turning the dial right down to zero. But as you say, the water kept on coming through.

Lomas

You should just turn it off at the mains. That'd be best.

Adele

I know, but I'm worried about the water situation – not having water to drink, and not being able to have a wash when I want to, and also the toilet.

Lomas

She was staring in bemusement at the water squirting out from beneath her thumb. When she asked me to do a stint for her, I said fine, and edged my thumb over the crack as she edged hers away. Our heads weren't close enough together for the question of hair smelling biscuity or not to be addressed with any precision, and the odour of rotten wood down by the floorboards was in any case quite strong – so, in a clumsy attempt to verify her identity, I asked her whether she'd had much trouble with plumbing in the past.

Adele

Hasn't everyone? It's dreadful – a constant worry. No matter how careful you are while cleaning – not banging pipes and so on – it's always going wrong. Springing leaks, exploding, or whatever.

Lomas

Showers, too, tend to lack reliability, I've found.

Adele

Yes, I remember; I believe you said so before. And then of course landlords, they exploit that whole popular myth about the scarcity of plumbers to ensure that weeks and weeks go by and nothing ever gets done. But sometimes you don't even call the landlord; you don't want strangers coming round to interfere with your appliances and talk to you, invading what's left of your privacy; you just want to be left alone. It doesn't matter how squalid and hazardous to your health your home has become. And that word 'home' is so revoltingly sentimental. Look at this place. Here there's nothing to sentimentalize. That's how I like it.

Lomas

Last time we spoke, you said you moved around a lot. I hadn't realized it was so regular.

Adele

It can be difficult – less so, now I own almost nothing. When I had lots of stuff, it was tricky, getting away at short notice and leaving no trace behind me. I needed help from time to time. Trying to get away from the Aldersons and Renton, I had this friend who got me out of the flat and organized a place to stay that was safe.

Lomas

That would be Crump.

Adele

He went to enormous pains to make sure it all went smoothly. We'd meet in arboretums and parks when we were planning it – always outdoors, so no-one could hear us and we wouldn't fall foul of the cameras in the flat. He was the only person who ever took me seriously when I told him about the cameras. And it worked, the diversion and all the other arrangements; we managed to fool them all, the Aldersons, my mother, Renton, we fooled them all completely. The only problem was, the diversion involved me driving a car when I hadn't driven for years and I'd lost my confidence as a driver.

Lomas

Yes, I've heard people say that before, about the confidence thing. Me, I found I slotted right back into it, the driving, like it was yesterday.

Adele

We had to do this switch with two hired cars. Up until that point it was fine, my driving was fine, but then I got lost en route to the halfway house and ended up on these winding country lanes, an absolute maze, and me going round and round in circles, and once I'd escaped from the country lanes there was this incident, almost an incident, on a busy dual carriageway, all these idiots driving too close, and me in a state... What I mean is, I nearly lost control of the car. And so I decided to find a hotel for the night. It wasn't part of the plan, but I needed a drink and some sleep and I'd noticed a suitably bland and anonymous venue just a few miles back, just before the dual carriageway. In the event it took me an hour to find it again, but I was lucky, there was a vacancy.

Lomas

Presumably you'd have been grateful for the facilities. Was it a chain hotel? The plumbing in chain hotels is often surprisingly good – robust, I mean – reliable – from what I recall of my travels.

Adele

I checked the toilet and shower to make sure they were clean, inspected the bedclothes for hairs and faeces – faecal particles, that's the giveaway – also beard hairs, freshly clipped beard hairs – and there's also dried menstrual blood – but it was spotless, actually everything was spotless, so I was pleased. Then I wandered down to the lounge and ordered a bottle of white wine. I planned to spend a few minutes poring over the road atlas, trying to work out where I'd gone wrong.

Lomas

Yes, it was always a bit of a treat, a bit of a luxury even, getting the chance to sit with a nice big drink and look at a road atlas. I always enjoyed doing that.

Adele

Unfortunately the lounge was full of conference delegates, braying and drunk, with lanyards round their necks. Some were flirting, others were boasting about their sexual exploits and mishaps; by the bar, one woman was thrusting out her backside and pulling the waistband of her thong up above her trousers so a male colleague could twang the string and sort of play it like a harp, except he yanked it up too hard and made her squeal. Quite a lot of the women were squealing, in fact, while most of the men were growling; there was one man who was vomiting into a fireplace, which I suppose was a kind of growling in itself, and there was another one crooning a song that had been popular a couple of years before, extolling the virtues of sexual prowess combined with constancy in a relationship. The noise was beginning to get to me; I thought about taking a walk, and I was looking out of the window, making sure it would be safe in the hotel grounds, when I saw this woman in the middle of the lawn. She was just standing there. She'd been gagged, and her wrists and ankles were bound with gaffer tape.

Lomas

Did you recognize her?

Adele

Not at all. Why do you ask?

100

Lomas

I'm not quite sure.

Adele

When I say she was standing there, she was at first – but then she kind of fell over. Something hit her on the head and she just crumpled. A couple of delegates walked past then, a man and a woman; they were holding hands and strolling down the path at the side of the lawn. I knocked on the window to get their attention, and I pointed. And they saw, they looked right at her, but they didn't stop to help; they went on walking. So I looked around and next I tried this middle-aged bloke who'd been standing near my table. He was wearing a lanyard and drinking like the rest, but he came across as slightly detached and projected an air of quiet authority. By the time I got him to look, they were pelting the woman outside with stones and empty beer cans.

Lomas

They?

Adele

Yes – the people attacking her. There was blood on her face by now, she looked bewildered, like she couldn't believe what was happening. So I yelled in this bloke's ear, I said we need to get some people together and get out there and help, but he just looked at me like he was dealing with an idiot or a hysteric, finally mumbling something, obviously a copout, to do with risk assessments or health and safety or something. Then he sloped away and managed to lose himself among his colleagues. By now the attackers had moved into view. There were five or possibly six of them, young blokes in their early twenties, and they'd gone from throwing cans and stones to throwing what looked like bolts. The woman was trying to crawl away. I got the attention of the barman and tried to make him understand we had an emergency on our hands. He said he'd phone and get security –

101

only he didn't, he just went back to pouring drinks out for the punters. I'd left my own phone up in my room, and there was no-one at reception, so I went outside and crouched behind a wall and tried to work up the courage to intervene myself. The problem was, I couldn't think what to say, I knew my voice would just seize up and then they'd laugh at me and come and get me too. They were laughing at the woman as I crouched there – and it was their laughter, the sound of their laughter, that made me realize something odd was going on.

Lomas

Their laughter was odd?

Adele

It sounded much too young for the men I'd seen through the window. And then I saw that some of the gang weren't men at all; they were teenage girls. And the ones that weren't were teenage boys.

Lomas

That is quite odd.

Adele

Also the woman had changed. She was moving, but not crawling like before. She was rolling, really slowly, on her side. She looked unnaturally shiny and smooth, and also pink, unnaturally pink, and in the moment just before she rolled out of sight I saw that the gang was made up of children – not even teenagers, just children – aged about nine or ten, maybe younger. They were helping her to roll by giving her gentle prods with their feet, and there was something in their manner that really disturbed me – something processional, even slightly reverential, as though they were taking part in a sacrificial rite. And what disturbed me even more was the knowledge that if I was seeing these children rolling a shiny smooth pink woman along with their feet, then maybe I

102

couldn't have seen those horrible men in their twenties throwing bolts at a woman who wasn't shiny and pink, and so maybe I wasn't seeing this either. It was just as well I hadn't called the police, because I might have ended up being charged or cautioned for wasting their time, or maybe they'd think I was totally nuts and get my mother involved – and so much, then, for the plan. So I went up to my room and found my tranquillizers, took a double dose with the rest of my wine, and that was me – quite fairly zonked beneath the covers.

Lomas

Despite the noise the braying delegates were making in the bar?

Adele

Yes, I had earplugs, and the tranquillizers were better than what I'd been used to. But I was still quite badly shaken when the effects wore off next morning, so I went straight out to look. The grass was wet, and there were bolts lying in it, and stones, and half a dozen empty beer cans. On the far side of the lawn there was a flowerbed; it was the last place I'd seen the woman, the place she'd rolled to when they'd been prodding her with their feet. I noticed that some of the flowers were crushed, and there was mud smeared on the gravel path beyond, leading up to a gap in a hedge that screened off where the hotel bins were stored. There was this awful smell: intensely sour and meaty, but not in the normal way that bins smell sour and meaty; this was stronger. There was blood on the ground. And then I saw the head, with its grinning mouth and staring eyes. A pig's head – not a person's head at all. And entrails everywhere. They'd butchered the poor beast clumsily. Actually, 'butchered' isn't right; it's not like they'd killed it for the meat. You could tell from the wounds – they'd tried to inflict as much distress as they could before it died. Nothing was taken except for the trotters. They'd left a cigarette stub protruding from one of its nostrils.

Lomas

Have you seen the children since?

Adele

No. I packed my things and got out of there as quickly as I could. I drove to the halfway house, as planned; then, when it was safe, I travelled onwards to the next place. Then another place after that. That's where you found me, in fact. When you came and asked about bailiffs and so on.

Lomas

So the unpleasantness at the hotel was…?

Adele

About three years ago. Slightly longer, perhaps. Four years.

Lomas

And you've been living in disused factories ever since?

Adele

Well, I know it's hardly perfect. But life's what you make it. I got a part-time job in a pub, a nice quiet pub, and for a short while nobody bothered me.

Lomas

You gave it up, the job. A person called Saoirse filled the vacancy.

Adele

I had no choice. My mother was close to tracking me down. One afternoon I saw a friend of hers outside the pub, in his car, with a map. He was making a phone call. I assumed the worst, and left. It was a shame, because those few months were almost pleasant. I used to cycle up to the moors to do my shift, and then I'd cycle back down and sleep in my quiet room in the disused factory. But you know about the time I spent at the pub. We arranged to meet there once. I waited. You didn't turn up.

Lomas

Yes, I'm sorry about that. I must have got confused about the arrangements. In my defence, I was ill at the time.

Adele

What was wrong with you?

Lomas

Myalgic encephalomyelitis. Trigeminal neuralgia. Necrotizing fasciitis. What about Crump – did he drink in that pub?

Adele

Just the once. He came to see me, but he was obviously quite depressed and couldn't bring himself to say much. Things were bad. You know, with Juniper's disappearance and all.

Lomas

Had you heard that she got better? Yes, she's doing rather well now.

Adele

Good. I'm glad. I always liked her, and I know how much she suffered. Both of them suffered.

Lomas

In that cottage? Because of the wind and rain and bad pointing?

Adele

It was more that they'd been cheated out of life. That's how he saw it, in my view. They'd both been in retreat for years. And then, when she vanished, there was nowhere left to go. I think what he wanted was to fade into the background, to have less im-pact – not by throwing all his stuff away, like before, but just by being less present, less tangible. That's what he wanted.

Lomas

Juniper said he sometimes made running away from life seem like a high political principle. Is it more akin to theology than politics, wanting to vanish?

Adele

You're making fun of him?

Lomas

On the contrary. I've been told that what he accomplished could serve as a beneficial example – not only to *Homo sapiens* generally, but specifically to me. I'm sure it speaks glowingly of his conviction and perseverance that he should go from getting rid of his possessions, as he did while he was with Constance, to effacing his very existence, or aspiring to.

Adele

He was applauded for throwing his junk away at the time. Maybe Constance wasn't impressed, but others admired him. Lots of people did it back then, for various reasons. It wasn't exclusively political.

Lomas

According to Constance, he mentioned shepherds' bothies, Anderson shelters, bivouacs and tents.

Adele

I'm not sure how he thought that would work. And it didn't work, did it? He ended up coming back into propertied life and setting up shop with Juniper. And when that went wrong, he already knew that running away didn't work, so he must have realized that another tactic was necessary. Which is why I say what he wanted was to fade into the background, to become less present and less tangible.

Lomas

What about silence? Did he want to live in absolute silence, like you?

Adele

I couldn't say. We didn't discuss it.

Lomas

You were a classically trained musician.

Adele

I used to screech in very high registers for a living. And it wasn't even a living. I wasn't good enough at it, the screeching, to make a living. Not in the sense of a regular income.

Lomas

You worked in a pub. It must have been noisy. Even on days when it was quiet. People make jokes. Machines play jingles. I know. I've been in pubs. A lot.

Adele

I had my pills to calm me down. And I was going through a good phase when I was working at the pub, which meant that the sounds didn't seem like manifestations of evil. When I'm bad, that's how they seem, the sounds that recreation and friendship make, the sounds of humour and music – they seem like manifestations of evil. Before you say anything, I'm aware of the implications. If I hate the noise of recreation and friendship, and if I hate music, which was formerly the centre of my life, then I hate life. And if I hate life… Well, I accepted long ago that there's a wish in me for death. Not a wish to die – the notion of dying really frightens me – but to be dead, to cut out the intervening unpleasantness and be dead. To become silence, nothing but silence. I know it's not a healthy way of thinking. During my good phases I'm drawn to less extreme solutions, like undergoing a surgical procedure that would nullify my hearing. I've looked into it, but no reputable doctor will do it. They don't take me seriously. Are you all right?

Lomas

It's the effort of stanching the leak. All this pressure against my thumb, it's making me nauseous.

Adele

Would you like the bowl to be sick in?

Lomas

I accepted her offer, but once she'd taken my place down by the radiator my nausea subsided; there was no need for me to vomit. Then, to move the conversation away from death, I mentioned her former routine of cycling up to the moors to do her shifts, and said I hadn't noticed a bicycle in the warehouse; had she lost interest, or given her bicycle away? The question seemed to make her uncomfortable; she immediately steered the discussion back towards Crump, whose political life, she explained, had been closely linked with the bicycle.

Adele

Yes, it started when he was ten or eleven; it started with this book he found on cycling. He just found it one day in a library.

Lomas

A public library?

Adele

Yes. I can't remember the title, but the book was full of iconoclastic perspectives on all sorts of things, ecology and society, even ethics and aesthetics, and it changed the way he thought about the world. So while the other boys were talking about some new sports car, he'd be stripping down his bike and then rebuilding it, or researching the environmental credentials of some new lubricant for chains. Everything that came afterwards grew from his reading of that book.

Lomas

You mean his achievements?

Adele

It depends on how you measure them. What I meant was… I don't know. Let's say his scepticism; his civilized refusal to conform. And his break with politics, too, his disillusionment with good old collective action – even that was linked with the bicycle, in a way. There was this incident – we were still at university – with this bunch of militant cyclists. He'd been shopping, and he'd come away with several bags of stuff, and he decided to get the bus, because it was heavy, the shopping; probably it was cutting into his hands. He'd been buying beer and potatoes, I recall, and probably carrots; he was really fond of carrots.

Lomas

Yes, they're decent, carrots. I like them. Celery, too.

Adele

So he was waiting at the bus stop, and he heard some kind of commotion up the high street. There was traffic in the distance, but nothing was moving. Then he noticed a block formation of hundreds of cyclists at the front. They were staging some kind of protest, something to do with reclaiming the streets from the evil hegemony of the internal combustion engine, which involved them pedalling slowly on their bikes while making parping sounds by blowing through kazoos and plastic trumpets.

Crump [box file]

And their protest was successful, in the sense that it brought the entire city centre to a halt and caused a massive accumulation of exhaust fumes and particulates that everyone with the misfortune to be waiting for a bus was forced to inhale. The militant cyclists, who were wearing the latest anti-pollution filter masks, could afford to piss their padded Lycra gussets with the hilarity of it, the ecstasy of unexpected triumph. Everyone else – the ones who didn't have enough money to run a car with air-conditioning, the elderly limping from day to day with concessionary passes, the deadwood with asthma and sight problems – they, as usual, were fucked.

Adele

He recognized a few of the biking crusaders – student radicals who'd be raking it in as high-profile human-rights lawyers or acquisitions-and-mergers consultants five years down the line. That was it for him, as far as organized action went. But he liked the symmetry of it, the way the bike had been there at the beginning and how it was still there at the end. He found it amusing.

Lomas

I'm sorry, I need to go to the toilet.

Adele

Down the corridor. Fourth on the right.

Lomas

Shall I shut off the water at the mains while I'm up?

Adele

To be honest, I don't know where the stopcock is.

Lomas

You should probably call a plumber, if you don't like dealing with landlords.

Adele

I haven't the time to stay in and wait. I've got an appointment. Were you bored by what I was telling you about Crump and the militant cyclists?

Lomas

No, it was good to hear about bikes. I used to be keen on cycling myself, when I was younger.

Adele

That doesn't surprise me. I get the feeling that the anecdote about Crump and the militant cyclists made you warm to him ever so slightly.

Lomas

This appointment of yours – where is it?

Adele

At the medical centre, first thing.

Lomas

I went to the toilet and had a bit of a think about what would be best to do next, and back in the room, when I'd started my next stint down by the radiator, I told her I'd be heading in the direction of the medical centre next morning. What I mean is that I offered her a lift, which she accepted.

Adele

I had the run of the place, within limits. There were several rooms I felt safe in. And with earplugs in, the sound of the leak didn't carry. So we abandoned it, the radiator, and went and got some sleep.

Lomas

It was next morning that my run of good fortune ended – back in the side street where I'd left Constance. There was a problem with the car.

Adele

What's wrong?

Lomas

It's not here.

Adele

What's not?

Lomas

The car.

Adele

Where's it gone?

Lomas

I don't know. Perhaps its owner came and reclaimed it.

Adele

It's not your car?

Lomas

I had it on loan. From someone called Saoirse. I think I mentioned her before. I kept it longer than I should have. Maybe she needed it for work, and got impatient, understandably so, and came and took it back.

Adele

At least you weren't here when she did. It could have turned ugly. She might have caused a terrible scene.

Lomas

This means I won't be able to give you the lift I promised, I'm afraid.

Adele

Don't worry. I'll walk.

Lomas

May I accompany you?

Adele

There's no need.

Lomas

It's on my way – the clinic, the medical centre, whatever you want to call it, it's on my way. That was where Constance was trying to get to when the children came and attacked her.

Adele

Children attacked her?

Lomas

Didn't I tell you about the children? I know I've left it rather late – checking up that she escaped, I mean – but that's why I need to go there, to the clinic, or the medical centre, whatever you want to call it. I want to check that she escaped.

Adele

Perhaps you should go to Saoirse's first and return the key. She must be relying on her spare. If she loses that, she'll be screwed.

Lomas

I know, but going on foot to Saoirse's, it'd take ages, and I'm more concerned about Constance. If you head off to the clinic by yourself, you might see Constance, or someone who closely resembles Constance, under attack from feral children. And then you might find a butchered pig in the patients' car park, or wherever they keep the bins, the staff at the clinic. I don't know where they keep the bins.

Adele

I'm sure she managed to deal with the children you mention. She used to be a teacher, you know. A strong, no-nonsense person — that's what Crump said. And if you're worried about mobility, why not get yourself a bike? There's a shop just round the corner where you can buy one fairly cheaply, if you don't mind second-hand.

Lomas

Are they properly reconditioned?

Adele

They look pretty much immaculate to me. With one of those bikes, you could do a sweep of the area quickly and put your mind at rest about Constance. Then you could go and find Saoirse and give her back her key.

Lomas

Eventually I found the shop; it took me all day, and the stock proved disappointing. Even the cheapest bikes were way beyond my means, and they'd been sloppily reconditioned: misaligned brake blocks, badly frayed gear cables, a preponderance of rust. It wasn't even a specialist bike shop, either; there were swords on display, and knives, and crossbows, and several replica handguns, making me wonder why she'd thought it worth recommending. I was annoyed with myself for wasting a day on such a foolish errand; I'd been naive, I realized, to think about buying a bicycle in the first place. Aside from the expense, there was the issue of selecting the right machine, the time and effort I'd have to devote to researching the current state of bicycle technology;

then, of course, there was the problem of the mild muscular atrophy I'd suffered during my illness, which had yet to be reversed. Cycling might well have a useful role to play in a structured programme of rehabilitative exercise, but in my weakened condition a strenuous ride to Saoirse's place might literally be the death of me: I could see myself having a funny turn in the saddle, falling off, and being crushed beneath the wheels of an HGV. I'd have to build up my strength in stages, perhaps by means of a vigorous walking routine, before I could seriously contemplate riding a bike again. And as for the money required to buy one, I was faced with a further problem: whether to make the process of raising the funds official. Doing casual work, unregistered with the authorities, went against my inclinations and would leave me liable to criminal prosecution; on the other hand, admitting to the receipt of taxable earnings would require that I declare myself to be resident somewhere, an occupant at a recognized address, a luxury currently denied me.

I decided to call Bettina, to ask her opinion. It would be awkward after such a protracted interval, but she'd sent me that message before, about making contact, so it seemed churlish not to try. Switching on my phone, I got no signal. I tried a public telephone further along the road, but the line was dead. I continued onwards, out of the town and into the countryside. Here, the two public telephones I came across – the ones, I mean, that hadn't been smashed up by vandals – rejected my coins. To check that my cash was still legal tender, I bought a pie and a cup of soup from a van at the roadside. The food wasn't cheap, but the man seemed happy to take my money.

I'd been rethinking my plan to go and look for Constance. Given that both of my recent visits to her had coincided with outrages committed against her person, I was coming round to the view that it would be prudent to defer another interview until my physical fitness had improved – and perhaps until I'd acquired a small selection of nonlethal weaponry, such as some pepper spray and a paintball gun. Besides, as Adele had pointed out, the real priority now was Saoirse. I was horrified by the thought of what I'd done – taking her car without her consent, and then exposing it to the possibility of an opportunistic theft by leaving it overnight in an undesirable area.

I lay down gingerly in the grass. A gentle rain was falling. Soothed, I took a moment to admire the colourful lichens encrusting the wall above my head. Some years before, I'd known the names, in English and Latin, of quite a few of the more common mosses and lichens, just as I'd known the names of quite a few of the more common European birds. Allowing everyday things to distract me, I'd lost a valuable body of knowledge. Was it too late for me to recover it? Relearning so many specialist words in English and Latin, and linking the words with visual images of the things they represented, would be a gargantuan task; it would take up a lot of my time. You had to balance these assumptions about the intrinsic value of knowledge with an assessment of its practical application. Still, I could look out for a reference book, a field book, and I could look out for some second-hand binoculars, and a waterproof sleeve for the book, and one of those rigid leather cases for the binoculars; that was within my capabilities, I could do that, it was within my capabilities, it would be good. I got to my feet and brushed myself down and resumed my journey. The rain had penetrated deep into my coat – and deeper still, into my bones, or into my muscles, or whatever it was that reacted with this dull, metallic ache when I placed a foot on the ground, or swung a limb for momentum, or raised my head to check the shifts and realignments of those vivid, useless impressions in the distance, vivid, useless impressions of overgrown verges, endlessly straggling dry-stone walls, and interlocked shadows of moors. Rheumatoid arthritis seemed like a plausible explanation, though I didn't know much about it other than what I'd overheard, some years before, from older people; in any case, my instincts told me that something like tendonitis would be a more realistic diagnosis, and that the whole issue of rain was diversionary. I didn't need a new or better coat, that much was certain. I'd owned this coat for twenty, twenty-five years; it was a faithful coat, and would probably last another twenty years, or twenty-five.

Up ahead, someone had erected a small tarpaulin work tent. Finding it unoccupied, I sat on the stool inside and waited for the rain to stop.

Lomas [box file]

We'd taken a day-trip to a historic English market town. The journey by train was surprisingly problem-free, and the first half-hour of mooching went smoothly, but while I was browsing through some lithographs in a shop, she wandered off. I went looking for her, and somehow happened to find myself in a small tarpaulin work tent concealing a hole in the ground that gave entry to a tunnel. It seemed plausible – to me, at the time, knowing her at the time – that she'd crawled into this tunnel; and so it followed that I should do likewise. I started on my hands and knees, but soon I was flat on my belly, using my toes and elbows to work my way forwards with shorter and shorter thrusts, until the tunnel became so narrow that no further progress was possible. This was good: it meant that she couldn't have come this way. She was thin, but not that thin. She hadn't crawled into this lightless tunnel to die; I'd overreacted. But now I was stuck. I couldn't go forwards; I couldn't go backwards. I should have been able to wriggle my way into reverse, but somehow I couldn't. I had crawled into a tunnel and now I was stuck.

The main thing that bothered me was the air quality, which was horrible. Otherwise, I felt a tremendous sense of calm. I knew that if I panicked I would suffocate; I would expand to fill the tunnel and that would be it for me – the end. And so I just lay there, trying my hardest not to laugh. And sure enough, after several minutes I felt my body start to contract within my clothes, shrinking into itself but apparently with no loss of strength or suppleness. Next I could move my arms a little; and then I could move my legs as well, enough to wriggle into reverse, to do what was necessary.

Later I found her drinking Earl Grey tea in a small but exclusive teashop. The proprietor took against me because my clothes were covered in filth, and while a cup of hot sweet tea would have gone down nicely after what I'd endured in the tunnel, I had to leave because she was threatening to call the police. Some weeks later I read a story in the paper about a heist in which a criminal gang had posed as engineers and dug a tunnel from a work tent into a bank vault or pharmacy cellar and made off with cash or drugs, but whether their tunnel was the one I'd wasted my time in, or risked my life in, or however you want to put it, I never found out.

6

Lomas

The journey to Saoirse's place took longer than it should have, and I made it longer by procrastinating. I was worried that our meeting would degenerate into what Adele had called a scene, with voices raised, uncomfortable questions, and the possibility of a further blow to the head. The weather slowed me down as well, and though I adapted my route to avoid the localized flooding, still I got soaked on a regular basis and kept on having to look for places where I could dry out my things without being asked to move on. When the weather was good, I'd spend the night on arable farmland or behind some roadside hedgerow, sleeping fitfully in the tent that was responsible for depleting my petty cash; when it was too windy or too wet to pitch the tent, I'd seek out a spot beneath a railway bridge or look out for a brick-built rural bus shelter that didn't smell of urine. In the course of my new routine I developed a working familiarity with covered markets, charity shops, soup kitchens and, once I'd arrived in Saoirse's town, the local public library. No-one befriended me; nor did I encounter too much casual abuse. I stayed on the edge of things, and in general I was left to conduct my business unmolested. Every so often I'd check my phone for network coverage, and eventually I managed to pick up a signal.

Bettina

What are you up to?

Lomas

Sleeping rough.

Bettina

What?

Lomas

Yes, it's part of the broader project.

Bettina

You're in a rut.

Lomas

Just biding my time.

Bettina

You're in a rut. You need to call in.

Lomas

Yes, you said. I got your message.

Bettina

What have you learned?

Lomas

How to keep warm. How to keep dry. How to avoid getting fully involved. I just listen – keeping my distance. That's how I learn about his movements.

Bettina

Have they offered you drugs at all?

Lomas

Who?

Bettina

The people you're with on the street.

Lomas

No. Why would they? I was offered a couple of sleeping pills at Constance's, but that had nothing to do with them, the homeless. They don't even notice me, most of the time.

Bettina

What do the homeless know about Crump?

Lomas

If you mention him, they just shake their heads and glare with superstitious gloom at their boots, if they've got boots, or at the ground. It's like you're breaking some kind of taboo. I'd say they view him as an outsider.

Bettina

And what about you?

Lomas

They view me as an outsider too, when they're aware of me. Mostly they aren't.

Bettina

I meant your health. It can't be healthy, what you're doing.

Lomas

I get by well enough. The public libraries, the soup kitchens, the charity shops… I've developed a decent routine.

Bettina

Soup kitchens. My God.

Lomas

No, it's interesting. It makes you think about things in a different way – things that lie beyond the narrow confines of the project. The charity that runs the soup kitchen has a religious affiliation, so I stand in the queue with my empty bowl and try to discern some trace of an overarching theology in the pinched and cryptic faces of the ladies who dole out the stew. But there isn't any – not that you can see. How could you discern traces of an over-arching theology by looking at someone's face? It does you no credit, thinking like that, subjecting ladies to such scrutiny, basing your thinking on what's probably a syllogistic fallacy or something similar. And then I find myself wondering – again – about the consolations of religion, from which I've always been excluded.

Bettina

The consolations of *religion*?

Lomas

From which I've always been excluded. Perhaps by genetic de-sign – that might be part of it – but more obviously by the crush-ing distaste I've always felt whenever I've come into contact with any form of doctrinal rhetoric.

Bettina

And now you think you've judged it too harshly?

Lomas

Not at all. It's truly contemptible. But so is most of the stuff that people like to believe. And I prefer to be open-minded. So I go back to the library and take a first step towards a more sym-pathetic understanding of the religious mind in action. I embark on an investigation of the great scholastic thinkers, paying es-pecially close attention to Anselm of Canterbury.

Bettina

Did that work?

Lomas

Not really. My interest in the topic began to wane. So I digressed into a study of the monastic orders of medieval Europe. I specialized briefly in the Cistercians, but didn't get very far with that either. Next I devoted my efforts to some stimulating research on the Romanesque churches of northern France.

Bettina

Northern France…

Lomas

I'd forgotten their names, the churches, the abbeys, the ones I saw on holiday, but I remembered how the architecture impressed me. It'd be good to go back, if I ever found the time. But I expect that there'd be problems with the language.

Bettina

What was it you liked about the architecture?

Lomas

The sense of paradox it presented. Glorification of the deity through… how shall I put it? The spatial effect, which was somehow inappropriate. The consecration of unending and absolute emptiness.

Bettina

Right.

Lomas

You said there was something urgent.

Bettina

In a way. It's to do with my tenure, here in this place. You need to call in.

Lomas

It wasn't the best of times for calling in. Two hours after hanging up on Bettina, I got my first sighting of Crump. He looked a bit older than the figure in the photograph I'd retained for verification purposes, but it was definitely him. He carried a rucksack, he was dressed in a worsted overcoat and a dark green fedora hat, and he was browsing through the overseas travel section in the library. I followed him that day – the first of several such days, each starting with the library and moving outwards through his various local haunts – but I found nothing especially noteworthy in his movements, either that day or on subsequent ones. He tended to spend less time in the covered markets than I did, and rather more in the train stations; otherwise, his daily itineraries weren't so different from mine.

Speaking to him was out of the question, of course. He'd arrived in the picture too late, and for the purposes of my enquiry he was already obsolete. Even following him was cheapening and distasteful; he didn't deserve it. His demeanour was that of a man who'd suffered some hardship – perhaps not great hardship, more likely a series of trifling hardships, revelations about his failure as a person among other persons, about his failure to withdraw from the world of people in a manner that would allow him to go on living with some dignity, something like that – and the fact that he was still present, consulting travel books in the library, was in my opinion a testament to something within him that demanded, if not respect, then at least the right to be left alone. But there was a problem. If Crump were known to be at large, if he could be sought out at will in the pub, or under a hedgerow, or behind the bins in some rat-infested back lane, where would that leave me? The attestants would be able to seek him out and settle whatever outstanding matters lay between them; the mystery would disintegrate, and then there'd be no pretext for continuing to draw on their respective situations and experiences. The focus of the project might have shifted away from Crump, but it was essential that he remain a missing person.

Perhaps his presence in the travel section meant that he was planning to leave the area; I hoped so, but until he left, my place was just behind him, just out of sight.

This resolution of mine was vindicated a few days after I'd taken it. Crump was sheltering in the doorway of a boarded-up and visibly rotting bookshop; I was a few yards down the street, affecting interest in the window display of a company selling repossessed white goods. That was when Saoirse appeared. She was trying to put her umbrella up, but it buckled in a gust of driving rain; instead of collapsing it and trying again, she threw it into the gutter, where the wind scooped it up and sent it skittering merrily down the road. Watching it go, she aimed a kick at a pile of refuse bags on the kerbside, but lost her balance and went sprawling in the rubbish.

If it hadn't been so early in the day, I might have assumed that she was returning home from an afternoon shift at the pub, except that a journey of such a length would have been impractical on foot, in such inappropriate shoes and such inclement weather. If she'd had access to a car, she wouldn't be wet, she wouldn't have lost her umbrella and fallen into the rubbish; her present misfortune was a direct result of the fact that I'd taken her car. I lumbered up to intercept her. My chest and shoulders hurt, and my knees. She took a step backwards.

Saoirse

What the bloody hell do you want?

Lomas

We had an appointment of sorts, remember? You were going to take me to visit some of your places.

Saoirse

Places?

Lomas

Places you used to go to.

Saoirse

What places? When?

Lomas

You didn't show me. I never found out.

Saoirse

What are you doing?

Lomas

I said there'd been trouble, major trouble, down the street, a great big fight involving petrol bombs and guns, and though it was clear she didn't entirely believe my story, she allowed herself to be ushered round the corner. As I'd hoped, the street we'd taken intersected with one of the long main roads that led down to the canal; five minutes later, we were splashing along the towpath. By the time the block of flats appeared through the rain, I'd mustered courage enough to ask about the car.

Saoirse

What in the name of Christ are you talking about?

Lomas

That, in some obscure way, made me feel that I'd been exculpated. Saoirse didn't think the topic worthy of discussion, and that was good enough for me. I didn't push it any further. Why try her patience?

Saoirse

We had an argument on the towpath. I lost my temper. I fell over trying to hit him. The new medication I was taking meant my balance wasn't too great.

126

Lomas

In fact she attacked me with a tree-branch, but she went
sprawling when I ducked out of the way. I don't remember what
I said that proved so offensive. I expected her to scramble up and
launch a second attack, but she just lay there in the mud, looking
tired and defeated. It occurred to me that if she'd had the energy
to come at me again, I might have had the opportunity to analyse
more closely the eyes and mouth, the sense of resentment and
disgust, the putative aptitude for hatred, and then I might have
formed an idea of how they related, if at all, to the expression I'd
seen on Constance's face when Constance had been struggling
with the children, how she'd frowned and set her jaw like a small
girl trying to wrest a toy back from an older child, a stronger
child, the sneering bully who'd seized it, not to mention the open
mouth with the straining black tongue and the two rows of
stumps where the teeth had crumbled. But I had no appetite for
combative tussling with others, male or female, so I wasn't disappointed when she chose to stay on the ground instead of re-
grouping. And simply working through the moral implications of
that momentary speculation had served a purpose, making it
clear just how distasteful and reductive it was to ransack individuals for traces of some attribute you'd formerly detected in
another. Which rather put vinegary versus biscuity into perspective, when I thought of it.

Saoirse

I didn't feel too good. I'd hurt my back. All I wanted was to get
home and have a hot bath.

Lomas

Perhaps those nights in the tent had depressed my constitution;
while I was shivering uncontrollably, Saoirse seemed largely unaffected by the drenching, even though she was covered in mud.
Up in the flat, she removed her shoes and coat and scarf, and took
a step forwards. Aware that I didn't smell too good, I took a step

backwards. Advancing another step, she began to inspect my face, as a veterinary surgeon might inspect the muzzle and jowls of an elderly dog suspected of harbouring cancerous tumours. A puddle of dirty water began to form around the clothes that she'd discarded. I thought I saw steam rising from the pile, but I couldn't be sure. As the flat was cold, it seemed unlikely.

Saoirse

I remember now. You were here to ask about Crump.

Lomas

Your flat was different last time I came.

Saoirse

Yes, the bastards put my rent up.

Lomas

Suddenly bored with the inspection, she turned away and sat on a heap of old bedclothes and curtains that seemed to function as a beanbag or banquette. From an adjacent heap, she dug out a bottle of liquor; after a decent swig, she passed it over to me.

Saoirse

When I couldn't afford the rent, the fuckers evicted me. I had to move up here. Everything's cheaper on this floor. It's good in a way, because it's drier than downstairs. Fewer leaks through the walls and ceiling.

Lomas

What she said appeared to be true, if only by virtue of the fact that the room was half the size of the one she'd had before. That was all there was to the flat: just a living room. At the foot of her mattress a cupboard supported a sink and a portable stove; opposite that, beyond a massive heap of clutter, was a partially screened-off corner in which an old metal bathtub stood next to a sinister-looking commode.

Saoirse

I need a hot bath. Pull the screen a bit further along. And pile those clothes against it. The least I can expect is a bit of privacy in my own flat.

Lomas

While I moved the clothes, she boiled up water by the kettleful, going back and forth to add it to the tub. When the tub was half-full, and the screen shored up by the laundry I'd shifted, she took a set of dry clothes and some towels, and edged through the gap I'd left at one end of the slope. From the other side, she instructed me to retreat.

Saoirse

Are you standing on the far side of the room?

Lomas

Yes, about halfway between the mattress and the door.

Saoirse

Good. I'm switching the bulb off now.

Lomas

After that, all that remained to light the room was the flame of a single candle somewhere on the other side of the screen. I heard the sound of a body sliding into water.

Saoirse

What can you see?

Lomas

The sink and the stove, or rather their outlines. May I have some more of this gin, or whatever it is?

Saoirse

As long as you promise you're not looking. I'm not some cheap and nasty stripper, you know. I'm not some skanky old whore to be peeped at and wanked over.

Lomas

Is it actually gin, this stuff? Only it tastes a bit unusual.

Saoirse

Never mind that. I know what you think. You think I'm easy. That's what you think.

Lomas

Sorry?

Saoirse

Easy. Loose. Promiscuous. You'll have been told that.

Lomas

Told by whom?

Saoirse

I don't know… Juniper. Adele, if you managed to find her. What did they tell you?

Lomas

What does it matter? I don't believe everything people tell me.

Saoirse

No, but you'd like to. All the prurient details, that's you. All the cheap thrills. You're a trader in gossip and filth. There's actually quite a strong whiff of the pimp about you. What did they actually tell you?

Lomas

What makes you think they told me anything?

Saoirse

There was a rumour going round. About me and my thing.

Lomas

What rumour was that?

Saoirse

Don't pretend they didn't tell you. Going in for a genital make-over or something; getting it done, and having it filmed, to get on the telly. An absolute slander. An absolute downright fucking lie.

Lomas

Well, now you mention it, it did seem rather far-fetched.

Saoirse

I wouldn't say that. People did. In fact a friend of mine, she went and did just that. She had it filmed. She had it broadcast. One of those shows about plastic surgery, body dysmorphia, sexual problems, one of those shows they used to broadcast late at night. She got her tits done, and her arse. Live on camera. Then her twat. She didn't really like the look of it, on account of its being lopsided and the lips hanging down too far. They filmed that too. She knew I wanted to get into journalism – serious journalism, stuff the mainstream media wouldn't touch – so she tried to get me involved. She thought a mission programme would be the best way in for me. She knew a thing or two about my condition, you see, which was getting worse and worse.

Lomas

Your condition?

Saoirse

Lichen sclerosus.

Lomas

Right.

Saoirse

My hole was closing up.

Lomas

Your hole?

Saoirse

My slit. I meant my slit. It was closing up.

Lomas

I'm sorry to hear it.

Saoirse

She said a mission programme on lichen sclerosus would fit in really well with something her contact at the production company was pitching. It would be great to raise awareness about such a little-known and highly distressing condition, she said, and in doing so I'd be helping other women. Well, I didn't care so much about other women; I was keen to break into the media, yes, but not like that, or not if I didn't have absolute control of the agenda. So I said no. But I kept thinking that doing something along those lines – something medical – it would be good for me, not least because it would force me to confront a set of taboos that had been damaging me for years. Did you notice what I said earlier? How I said 'my hole' and 'my slit'? That's a major psychological achievement for me.

Lomas

Really? Congratulations.

Saoirse

No, but it is. For years I couldn't actually bring myself to use the personal pronoun in relation to those body parts, the ones to do with sex. I wasn't a prude; I just had this thing where somehow I wasn't able to talk about those body parts as mine – like I was ashamed to publish ownership of my own body. And the form it took, that shame, was using the definite article instead of the personal pronoun. That doesn't work, of course. The French don't use the personal pronoun; they use the definite article, and no-one accuses the French of being prudes or being ashamed to publish ownership of their own bodies. 'Have you a condom at the hand?' That's the construction you'd use in French. Then of course you've got the Germans, with the German fondness for nudism, and Germans use the definite article too. 'I wash to myself the hands', say, or 'I comb to myself the hair'. What it meant was – in reality, I mean – when I was having sex with some bloke, and he wanted to know how to get me going, or finish me off, I had to instruct him in this stilted way that relied on saying 'the' instead of 'my'.

Lomas

That must have been awkward.

Saoirse

And the story was the same when I went to the doctor's, when they wanted to know where it hurt, or where the problem was, or where the problem wasn't. Below 'my back', there were 'the buttocks' and 'the anus'; above 'my knees', I had 'the vulva' and 'the thighs'. The funny thing was, when it came to sex, I was always broadminded; I'd tried most of the things you could do without risk of putting yourself in an ambulance, and I'd liked them, and I didn't have any major physical hang-ups, so when it came to this thing with the pronouns I thought I'd identified a discrepancy. One that ought to be corrected. But with absolute control of the agenda.

Lomas

Did you manage that? Getting control of the agenda?

Saoirse

Up to a point. I decided to do a video diary.

Lomas

I remember those.

Saoirse

I thought it would help me through the experience. More importantly, if it went well, I thought I might be able to use the footage as part of a large-scale piece of conceptual art. That was my thing at the time, as well as doing the journalism: I was trying to establish myself as a multimedia artist. And because it was just me, the video diary – no production crew, just me and sometimes a doctor or sometimes a nurse – I thought everything would come good when I started filming, and the words would just fall into place. Only they didn't. I couldn't say anything. You can imagine how much worse it would have been if I'd taken Trudy's advice and gone through that on the telly.

Lomas

Would it have made it as far as the telly?

Saoirse

I think the company went bust before the new series got to the editing suite. But that's not the point. Just taking part in the thing would have traumatized me. Trying for words and failing, while the film crew stood round impatiently. The whole thing would have been terrible. Does my prudishness surprise you?

Lomas

I thought you said it wasn't prudishness.

Saoirse

Don't quibble. Just be honest. It surprises you. You had me down as someone who didn't care what other people thought. The sort of girl who could say whatever she liked about her body and just not care. Is that what you thought?

Lomas

I hadn't really formed an opinion.

Saoirse

Well, if you thought that, you'd be wrong. And when it comes to the personal pronouns, I'm still pretty fucked up and disassociated about it. I might be able to say 'my slit' and 'my hole' or whatever, but that's really as far as it goes. I still can't manage the clinical terms. And I know why you're not saying much. You can't handle the fact that I'm throwing in terms like 'personal pronoun' and 'definite article' and 'French construction' and using them correctly. It doesn't square with what you've heard about me, using terms like that with such authority and confidence. Am I right?

Lomas

I hadn't really formed an opinion.

Saoirse

You might be interested to know that I was once a published poet. Ten, fifteen years ago. In little magazines. Very specialized, very select. That's all finished with now, but I'd like to think my brain hasn't turned completely into shit.

Lomas

The sound of splashing water drowned out her next words, so I clambered up the soft embankment of clothing, often sinking, occasionally having to rebuild it as I progressed, until I was level with the top of the screen, where a meshed horizontal panel obscured my view of the bather while letting me hear her voice with greater clarity. Just after I got there, however, the sound of splashing water ceased and her monologue came to an end.

Saoirse

A paradox, that's what it was. You couldn't say anything against it, and the harder you tried, the stupider you seemed. You had to join in. You just had to grin and bend over and take it. Every crass little thing, every crass little shittiness anyone ever invented — you had to buy into it, or else they'd fucking well have you. No wonder some of us felt that any culture worth having was already dead.

Lomas

As I'd feared, this didn't leave me much to work with. So I did my best to bluff, asking her what she thought was left to her in the absence of it, any culture worth having.

Saoirse

What do you mean? What does that mean?

Lomas

Well, if the culture was already dead… what did you do?

Saoirse

Weren't you listening?

Lomas

Yes, intently. But what struck me was the contrast between confessional telly and diaries, video diaries, on the one hand, and the world of small-press poetry on the other. So that's, you know, what I was asking about.

Saoirse

And that's what I was telling you about.

Lomas

Yes, but I was also struck by the contrast between the video diaries and poetry on the one hand, and Crump's corporeal aspirations on the other. With respect to self-exposure, I mean.

Saoirse

Corporeal aspirations? What in the name of fuck are you talking about?

Lomas

Crump. He wanted to fade into the background. He wanted to be less present, less tangible.

Saoirse

Who told you that?

Lomas

Just something I heard. In addition, there was something to do with fear.

Saoirse

And you think turning into a cloud of dispersing atoms was how he wanted to deal with his fear? You think it's got something to do with his legendary and frankly now quite boring disappearance?

Lomas

I don't know. What do you think?

Saoirse

I think you've been spending time with Adele. No-one else could have come up with anything so crassly disingenuous. You've been taken right in there.

Lomas

Taken in?

Saoirse

Do you honestly want to know about Crump's fear?

Lomas

I honestly do.

Saoirse

Well, here's what it is. Here's a juicy bit of motive. Juniper's moping about in bed one day, pretending to be dying, and Crump's out running some stupid errand in her car. He's stuck at a junction in town, the traffic's backed up, nothing's moving, and there's some meathead in the car behind who thinks because the car in front isn't moving the fact that nothing's moving has to be the fault of whoever's in front. So this meathead starts flashing his headlights and sounding his horn and waving his arms about like a dickhead. Next he's revving his engine, lurching forward, braking hard, reversing a bit, then revving his engine, lurching forward, braking again… He's lost control completely, he's making an absolute exhibition of himself, and it seems to Crump that this person has forfeited any right he might have had to exist in a civilized society. So he gets out of the car, he's got the wheel-lock in his hand, and with the butt of the wheel-lock he smashes the meathead's face in.

Lomas

And this meathead, did he live?

Saoirse

I think he made a full recovery in the end. But Crump didn't know that when he went missing. When he went missing, it was still looking fairly bad. There was a police investigation, it made the news, and he assumed that there'd be witnesses coming forward, or there'd be footage of the assault. And after Juniper's disappearance, with the police on the scene, he was sure they'd make a connection and arrest him.

Lomas

I'd been paying such close attention to what she was saying that it came as quite a shock to find I'd fallen asleep and rolled down to the bottom of the slope. Saoirse was sitting on the mattress, dressed in a towelling robe and bed socks, with a fur hunting cap on her head. I tried hard to look alert, but I couldn't concentrate. When I woke up again, she was pottering at the sink, and somewhat later she was busy behind the partition. I heard metal scraping on floorboards, the sound of the window being opened, the distant crash of bathwater hitting the ground outside. Saoirse glanced at me occasionally as she moved around the flat. I thought I sensed her disapproval. Then it was morning and she was gone.

I decided to risk a bath, but made it quick, just two or three inches of cold water in the tub, which I then poured out of the window. Rifling through the landslide of rumpled clothes, I found some bed socks which were large enough for my feet, a pair of French knickers that would suffice as a pair of underpants, and a nightgown that would double as a T-shirt. All were clean. Just before leaving, I slipped the car key under her pillow.

I didn't see Crump any more after that. I gave it another few weeks – poking round in the stations, in the alleyways, under the railway arches – but nothing. It seemed he'd moved on. It seemed that I too should move on.

7

Lomas

Bettina?

Bettina

Who's there?

Lomas

It's me.

Bettina

Are you sure? I wasn't expecting to hear from you again. What's going on?

Lomas

Not much. Almost nothing.

Bettina

Is that a productive use of your time?

Lomas

Not really, no. I'm getting sick of it, to be honest. Not enjoying it. Want to get out.

Bettina

Out in what sense?

Lomas

You know – like that other bloke did. The legal bloke. Or was he something in finance.

140

Bettina

He was pretty high up in accounts, I think you said.

Lomas

And he just chucked it all in, remember? He just chucked it all in and went, he just got going, and things worked out for him just fine. A nice quiet life up a rural valley somewhere, no neighbours for a quarter of a mile, a bit of carpentry in the mornings, a couple of hens roaming out in the garden, a glass of pinot noir at lunchtime, or was he a beer man? No problems with people messing him about, no problems with money. He wasn't much older than I am now.

Bettina

With him it was different. He didn't procrastinate like you did. That's what you told me. And he was good with people. He knew how to deal with people. He could get them to do what he wanted.

Lomas

Yes… that's right. Yes, I knew there was a reason.

Bettina

Listen. I know this is hardly the time, and it would've been better if you'd been able to call in, but while you're on the line I might as well let you know. There's been talk of having you take on some extra responsibilities.

Lomas

I don't understand.

Bettina

Given everything that's happened.

Lomas

I didn't know anything had happened.

Bettina

There's been some unpleasantness.

Lomas

To do with what?

Bettina

To do with me, but that's hardly important. I'm getting quite used to it. Can you come in?

Lomas

I didn't feel up to going in. I went to see Juniper instead. She wasn't at home when I called, so I settled down to wait outside her flat. The front door had been redecorated since my last visit, but someone had already used a black marker pen to vandalize the new paint job, showing a disembodied penis, from which depended a cactus-like scrotum, entering a disembodied vagina, to which was appended a tuft of pubic hair and a tightly puckered anus. Threatening messages had been scrawled across the door and the brickwork surrounding it, things like 'vinegar tits' and 'kill bitch fucking grass'. Then there was the smell, a terrible smell accompanied by overlapping stains, which seemed to confirm that the front of Juniper's home had been employed as a public urinal.

Backed up in a corner, sitting as far as I could from the urine, I checked my phone at regular intervals. After six or seven hours, I got enough of a signal to send her a message – just enquiring after her health and suggesting a meeting. Her reply was eight days in coming; by then, I was in the middle of sorting out my financial situation. The message directed me to a department store ten miles away.

Juniper

Premises in mothballs, having to tidy up for sale. Come to rear entrance, one marked loading bay, use intercom. Will buzz you up. Love, J.

Lomas

I set off as soon as my shift was finished, but didn't make very quick progress as the extra weight of my leafleting sack cut into my shoulder and didn't sit well with my rucksack. It was evening by the time I arrived, though Juniper hadn't yet left. She buzzed me in and said to make my way straight up to the director's office, top floor. I found the main stairway, a vast and grandiose construction in ersatz marble, and started to climb. Successive landings gave glimpses of murky shop floors with nothing much in them but packing crates, nude shop dummies, and hangers on clothes racks. On the eighteenth floor the stairway came to an end at a windowless fire door. Beyond was a landing with a second door, slightly ajar, revealing a narrow section of office space.

Juniper

Come in, if you can. I can't move round much at the moment, I'm afraid. I'm in the middle of something. Sorry.

Lomas

Squeezing through the gap, I clambered up and sat on the desk that blocked the doorway. The office was cluttered: metal filing cabinets, sacks of shredded paperwork, old cash tills with circular keys, beyond which Juniper could be seen in a cupboard or recess. Only her face and hands were visible; the rest of her was obscured by a squat grey filing cabinet. On top of this were papers, which her hands were sifting and sorting with expert rapidity. The recess appeared to be packed with files and boxes, leaving barely enough room for a person to fit inside, and it was partly concealed by a concertina-style door, the kind I associated with continental hotels, especially French hotels, in films I'd seen long ago.

Juniper

Sorry again about the mess. I'm clearing old documents out and so on, to get it ready for the buyers. What about you?

Lomas

Me?

Juniper

You're doing something business-related yourself, to judge by your livery.

Lomas

Oh... I came here straight from work. Delivering leaflets, door to door.

Juniper

You mean you're losing interest in Crump? That surprises me. You seemed like a tenacious sort, the sort who wouldn't give up. What are you doing? Branching out into public relations?

Lomas

No, it's just casual stuff, part time.

Juniper

So you're not giving up on Crump?

Lomas

No, I just need some cash for expenses.

Juniper

And have you made much progress on Crump?

Lomas

I've had some financial problems. They're more or less sorted now.

Juniper

How many people have you spoken to?

Lomas

It's tricky. I need a permanent address, or at least a forwarding address.

Juniper

How many people?

Lomas

Not many.

Juniper

His male friends?

Lomas

No. Just Saoirse, Adele and Constance. And of course you.

Juniper

So what have you found out, talking to Saoirse, Adele and Constance, and of course me?

Lomas

Mainly stuff to do with fear.

Juniper

What fear?

Lomas

Crump's fear.

Juniper

And what have you learned about Crump's fear? That I was to blame?

Lomas

I wouldn't say that. In fact, it was put to me that his fear predated not only your connection with him – your shared domestic arrangement – but also his first encounter with Saoirse. It had something to do with lives being yoked together in property – *sanctified* by property – and the horror of existence as endured by cohabitees.

Juniper

And the suggestion is he vanished because of this fear? Where could he have gone where it wouldn't have followed him?

Lomas

There was also a suggestion that he was capable of sudden bursts of anger.

Juniper

Isn't everyone?

Lomas

Yes, but the theory is that he feared the possible consequences of some of those bursts of anger. One in particular. I don't know whether it's true, but that's what I heard.

Juniper

Look. I don't know who told you what, and to tell you the truth I'm not that interested, but let me just remind you that I lived with Crump for eight years and during that time I got to know him pretty well. So I can assure you with a fair degree of authority that his anger was nothing to speak of. As for his fear – let's call it anxiety instead – less melodramatic – if his anxiety had an identifiable source, it was an excessive supply of empathy, not an excessive supply of anger. He was swamped in moral relativism; he'd be able to see so many different sides to most moral questions that he wouldn't know what to think about them, much less what to do. In a way, it ruined his ability to function as an active social being. Don't get me wrong, I'm not suggesting he was… I don't know, an immoralist, something like that. He didn't lack a code of ethics. Quite the opposite, in fact. It was because he couldn't bring himself to judge people, to demonize them or write them off as scum, that he was *unable* to do any sudden bursts of anger. He couldn't get worked up to the extent that he could shout at people or hit them. If he got angry, it never went anywhere but inwards. Have you still got that thing with you, that box file?

Lomas
I used a standard lamp to push it over the dusty tops of the filing cabinets blocking the way between us. Intercepting it, she flipped the lid and thumbed through.

Juniper
So, then. What do you say to this?

Lomas
Using a golf club, she pushed the box file back towards me. The sheet of paper she'd selected was at the top.

Crump [box file]
This quantum of self, what is it? Not what it was. A schoolboy project which, until recently, I still tinkered with at weekends, now fit for the scrapheap. I have squandered what my younger self passed on to me; is it reasonable to feel guilt about that loss? Viewed statistically, existence is miraculous; the odds against being born are truly incalculable; one's life is several billions of years in the making, yes – but where is the place of morality in

this? Is the moral dimension intrinsic or simply imposed? Matter is disparate, comes together, forms a thing, and is then destroyed, or, put more neutrally, transformed. Why encumber the process of wastage with spurious notions of duty and guilt?

Juniper

Hardly the voice of some raging psychopath, is it?

Lomas

No – though you could argue that while it's fairly uncontroversial to conceive of life as a brief convergence of matter, it isn't entirely inconsistent with the mind-set of a psychopath to dislocate the wastage of it, that brief convergence of matter, from the moral dimensions of duty and guilt that otherwise might preserve it. But I'm not the one to propagate such a thesis.

Juniper

You're too swamped in moral relativism?

Lomas

No, not really. I'm just not the one to attempt it.

Juniper

What else did they tell you?

Lomas

Who?

Juniper

The others.

Lomas

Oh... too early to draw conclusions. I haven't verified the data. Haven't had time.

Juniper

What about Saoirse? What did she tell you?

Lomas

This and that. As I just said –

Juniper

Did you like her?

Lomas

Well… we rubbed along nicely enough.

Juniper

I'll bet you did.

Lomas

We planned to visit some of the places they used to go. Saoirse and Crump, I mean, the places they used to go. You know, days out. It didn't happen, though – not that day. She didn't take me. We didn't get round to it.

Juniper

She stood you up. She dropped you in the shit.

Lomas

It was more that she couldn't make it on the day, I believe. I think she had other commitments.

Juniper

Well, I won't be able to help with that, I'm afraid. Not today, and probably not for the rest of this month.

Lomas

Help with what?

Juniper

Doing the places. Visiting places he used to go. The sorts of place he might have gone to disappear from. I can't afford to go traipsing all around the countryside when I've got this ton of paperwork to deal with. But if he really did make his way to one of those places of his and then wander off into the distance, I'd be intrigued to know how he managed to square doing that with what he believed about making a satisfactory ending. Lazy endings really offended him. He hated films and novels and TV dramas where there's a pairing off at the end, as though dumping two people together in bed or trotting them out in front of a vicar is going to save them from the horror of what's coming next — the localized horror of two human lives going slowly putrid in an aluminium can. He could be grumpy like that when it came to popular culture. The problem for him, though, was that even the lack of an easy resolution wasn't good enough — not, at least, if it smacked of the sentimental gesture, like it would if some tragic hero wandered glumly into the distance. That'd be just as much a cop-out as the tearing off of the clothes, the cheek nestling happily on the chest-hair, the giggling maids and fine young bucks lined up in church with the rheumy old cleric. Like I said, he could be grumpy. When he was younger, it was enough for him, the distance and what it implied, how it seemed like something you could escape into. But the older he got, the less it seemed to work. One day we went hiking, and when we were halfway up the mountain, he got this pain in his chest, and then he started to vomit. He wouldn't tell me what the problem was. We'd been stuck in a traffic jam earlier, which had been stressful — we'd witnessed a fight — but that wasn't it. I just kind of sensed he had this horror of being out there in the open; something was after him, and fresh air and the horizon didn't make his feeling of being pursued any easier. We didn't go hiking much after that. I wonder if he remembered that, when he finally wandered off, or made his plans to wander off.

Lomas

Perhaps the box file will turn something up. Shall I pass it across?

Juniper

What for?

Lomas

You seem to have a knack with it.

Juniper

Try having a rummage yourself.

Lomas

I did as she said, selecting a document at random.

Crump [box file]

When I was contemplating leaving, leaving for good, I looked at the options and found there was nowhere left to go. Nor was there anywhere left to stay. And yet there was nowhere left to go. And still my rucksack stood in the doorway, a *fait accompli*, exuding impatience, more accusatory than any inanimate object had any right to be. I should have set fire to that rucksack. I did consider it – I even got as far as fetching the matches and some methylated spirit – but pity stopped me. Pity for a rucksack and its contents: proof that my human existence was finished.

Juniper

Anything significant?

Lomas

Something about there being nowhere left to go.

Juniper

Does that make it more likely that he wandered off into the distance? Or less?

Lomas

What do you think?

Juniper

You know what I think. I told you before. I think he's dead.

Lomas

Or close to death. That's what you said.

Juniper

Yes, but how long can you go on being close to death? He must be dead by now. Or if he's hanging on, he can't have long to go. Perhaps he's waiting for something to happen first.

Lomas

Given that I'd seen him walking the streets a few weeks earlier, it seemed mean to let Juniper go on thinking that Crump was close to death, or dead, or undergoing some kind of karmic transformation, or whatever it was she believed. On the other hand, if I told her he was alive, she'd want to know why I hadn't mentioned the fact straight away, and that would be it: I'd lose whatever limited influence I had with her, precisely at the point when I needed to call on her for practical assistance.

Juniper

What do *you* think it is?

Lomas

Sorry?

Juniper

What do you think it is that needs to happen before, you know, he can die?

Lomas

I don't share your certainty that he is about to die.

Juniper

So why are you here?

Lomas

I don't follow your logic.

Juniper

Sometimes I think that you… oh, forget it.

Lomas

No, please go on.

Juniper

Let's just say that you give off a *lot* of negative energy. You should try some spiritual healing.

Lomas

Thanks, that's useful. I'll bear that in mind. But first there's a rather delicate matter I need to raise. It has to do with my financial situation. I touched on it earlier.

Juniper

You want to make use of my address?

Lomas

Purely for contact purposes.

Juniper

Contact involving whom?

Lomas

Potential employers. The authorities.

Juniper

So from an official point of view there'd be an assumption that we were cohabiting?

Lomas

No, I wouldn't put it like that. Not cohabiting. Not exactly.

Juniper

Sorry. I'd like to help, really I would. But it's not convenient just now. Even pretending would make things too complicated. I've got someone coming to stay. Moving in with me for a while. A very good friend.

Lomas

Anyone I know?

Juniper

How could it be someone you know? What people do both of us know?

Lomas

Do you still have the cat?

Juniper

You're changing the subject. Why would that be?

Lomas

I'm not very good at intrusive questioning. It brings on my globus pharyngis. And my eczema. Not to mention various other psy-chosomatic disorders I'm prone to. Mucoceles, too — from chewing the inside of my lip. Intrusive questioning makes me chew the inside of my lip.

Juniper

You're happy to imagine me living with a cat, but inviting a person to stay with me puts me beyond the pale?

Lomas

I found the cat soothing to watch. My enquiry related exclusively to its welfare.

Juniper

You think I'm one of those desperate, sexless old spinsters, whose fingers…

Lomas

I never mentioned your fingers. Your fingers are no concern of mine.

Juniper

Well, let me tell you. Just before Saoirse seduced him – Crump – before I got ill – something happened. Almost happened. I was very nearly unfaithful to him; I almost went off with a man. A man I worked with. At a party, it was. We'd had a lot to drink. There'd been some pleasant conversation, just me and him, and something just clicked. I'd been aware of it for some time, this connection between us, but naturally I'd said nothing; I wasn't the type, I wasn't some tart who went off with anyone, I was with Crump and that was just the way it was. But that night it was different. The conversation was flowing freely; I was enjoying it more than I'd enjoyed being with another person for ages; simply being together, two people finding pleasure and ease in each other. And towards the end of the evening, as he was saying goodbye, he touched me on the forearm. An affectionate gesture, not remotely calculated; barely even a touch. Perhaps he didn't touch me at all, or not on the skin; perhaps I already had my coat on and he just lightly brushed my sleeve. But whether he touched me or not, what it meant… it didn't go further, but still… a random touch on the arm; I couldn't stop thinking about it. Afterwards I felt melancholy and strange. It was most unlike me;

everything seemed different. I'd go for long walks in bad weather, and listen to madrigals, which I hadn't done for years. And
I felt terribly sad for Crump. I felt sad for our shared existence.
But what made me saddest of all was the knowledge that I
wouldn't have been able to go with him, the man at the party,
even if I'd wanted to – that, and the fact that I kept on actually
wanting to believe that I might have been able to. That stupid
contradiction, and my failure to resolve it – that was what made
me sad.

Lomas

I didn't know what to say to this, so I nodded in what I hoped
was a wise and experienced sort of way and made some remark
about how late it was and how I needed to go.

Juniper

It's not him, by the way. The person who's coming to stay with
me, the friend – it's not that man I've just been telling you about,
who touched me on the arm. And look, if you're really desperate
for somewhere to stay, there's no reason why you shouldn't have
the old storeroom – next landing down.

Lomas

That's very decent of you. Thanks.

Juniper

If you didn't already have the job with the leaflets, I might have
asked you to help me out with the tidying up. But then again, I
probably wouldn't have been able to pay you very much, so
you're probably better off as you are. There was no money in the
will, you see, just the building. My uncle was skint; I hadn't seen
the old bugger for decades but I knew that the business had
already pretty much folded by the time he finally drank himself
to death. It's hardly a *deus ex machina*, my inheritance, despite
what you might think. I've got all my uncle's debts to pay off,

and I'm too much in debt myself, what with the mortgage on the flat, to make a huge profit from the sale. I bought when prices were really scandalously high; the cottage was derelict, as you know, and so the developers felt they could rip me off, and I let them. There was a gap of several weeks before I found the flat, and meanwhile prices were rising by the hour, they were practically doubling overnight… I almost ended up with nothing. Even if I get a good price on this place, there'll be precious little left once I've paid it all off. Do you want to know how truly pathetic I am, how grossly materialistic? When the news of my uncle's death came through, the first thing I thought was how fantastic it would be; how once I'd sold it all off, I'd be able to buy a place abroad, perhaps in the French Pyrenees, the Swiss Alps, the Italian Lakes, or even a place in all three. Now it's looking as though I might just be able to stretch to a fortnight's holiday in each. But this is undignified; you don't need to listen to this, you've got enough problems of your own. Let's get you some keys. I'll show you the storeroom.

8

Lomas

A further visit to Constance now seemed both justified and time-ly, but my leafleting schedule was currently so demanding that I had trouble getting away. When I did secure a free weekend, my journey to her flat was hampered by injury: a stabbing pain in my groin that forced me to stop at regular intervals, sitting down with my legs spread out until the worst of the pangs had subsided. It might have been nothing more than a simple muscular strain, but given the volume and weight of what I'd been lugging around in recent weeks, I couldn't help favouring a more sinister diag-nosis: inguinal hernia was the obvious one, though I couldn't actually feel my bowel protruding into my scrotum. As a result of the moderate pace I felt it prudent to adopt, it was almost dark when I reached the square where Constance lived. She didn't answer immediately, coming to the door only after I'd rung the bell five or six times. Again she was wearing the brown-and-orange housecoat, but now it was complemented by a black woollen shawl, a black velour beret, and jam-jar sunglasses with thick brown plastic frames. Once I'd convinced her that I was indeed the person I claimed to be, she welcomed me with an enthusiasm I hadn't been expecting.

Constance

We could do with someone like you around. It's long overdue.

Lomas

Someone like me?

Constance

Yes, who can knock a few heads together.

Lomas

You're sure about that? You really see me in that role?

Constance

Of course. And you shouldn't be so diffident. Pissing about like that, refusing to take a stand, that's half the problem. That's how they think they can get away with it. Have you seen the state of the walls?

Lomas

Expletives had been daubed in thick black paint above the dado rail. It looked as though Constance had applied several coats of emulsion in an attempt to cover the offending material, but whatever she'd used had been of such poor quality that it barely made any difference. I wasn't sure what conclusions I was meant to draw from the evidence, so I just asked a few pertinent questions – in the manner, I suppose, of an insurance loss adjuster.

Constance

He was quite good to have around that day, in retrospect. He tried to do the right thing. My nerves were shredded, though, and I probably wasn't as nice to him as I should have been. I told him how much worse the situation had got since his previous visit.

Lomas

Did someone break in?

Constance

No.

Lomas

Did a guest run amok?

Constance

Not at all.

Lomas

Did you run out of paint?

Constance

No, I kept on getting distracted by all that bloody noise from next door. I lost my temper and painted obscenities on the wall. Listen to that.

Lomas

What am I listening for?

Constance

Creaking sounds. They've changed since the last time you came. One of the problems is I've learned to interpret them better; I've honed my translational skills, and now I can pick out the details.

Lomas

That can't be good.

Constance

I've got no problem with people swamping themselves in filth. It's when I can hear it through the walls that I object. And I'm not some rabid curtain-twitcher, either. The lives of other people don't interest me that much; I'd rather they just kept themselves to themselves. I didn't even know she had a child until last month. When I say a child, I mean a son in his early teens – a boisterous prick.

Lomas

You worked that out from the creaking?

Constance

Yes, and the swearing. And shortly afterwards, a larger, bulkier presence moved in: her latest beau, I presumed, or maybe her pimp. Is that unkind? I know she's feckless but I don't think she's a prostitute. Anyway, this bloke, her conjectural beau, I started to notice him out in the square, a bloody great beefcake with these pornographic tattoos on his arms and chest. You'd see him several times a day, as though he had business affairs that kept taking him elsewhere – selling drugs, breaking kneecaps, trafficking teenage girls from abroad, that sort of thing. She threw a party one evening last week – out the back, where she had no right to, the shared back yard. She had all sorts in, coming and going, including the bloke with the porno tattoos, and from the way he acted and moved around I could tell that his was the larger, bulkier presence I'd been hearing through the wall. Others coming and going had their kids with them. They all got horribly drunk, the kids included, and by dawn next day they sounded barely human. Whenever I went to the toilet, or tried to, they'd bawl some offensive remark or lob something up at the window, except that most of the time I couldn't use the toilet; I was too self-conscious and overwrought. In the end I opened the window and started haranguing them. It was the beau who copped the worst of it – most of the guests had already gone – but I think the woman was in earshot when I said it. She was wandering in and out of the yard, looking for her knickers. And I said to him, the bloke, I said you're scum and so is she, the whole fucking lot of you are, the whole fucking stinking shit-puddle, you and your ignorant slut and her wank-faced brat of a son, why don't you fuck off back to the slum where you belong, fuck off and die in your own shit. You people are nothing, you contribute nothing, you're a worthless heap of piss, there should be camps for rubbish like you.

Lomas

You actually said that?

Constance

No, not all of it. I was too angry. I just told them that they con-
tributed nothing. The rest of the words wouldn't come.

Lomas

At least it's fairly quiet now.

Constance

You think so?

Lomas

Don't you?

Constance

It doesn't actually make any difference. It could be silent, utterly
silent, deathly silent, and still I'd be waiting for the next creak.
And I know that creaks are only creaks; it's what they presage
that stops you from sleeping at night, and that's what ruins your
life.

Lomas

I don't know what to suggest.

Constance

You could have them killed.

Lomas

What?

Constance

Don't tell me you couldn't arrange it.

Lomas

To have them killed?

Constance

You've been around. You've seen some action. Your face has been lived in. It's got a lived-in look or quality.

Lomas

Well, I admit my career trajectory hasn't been the most stratospheric –

Constance

It's the face of a man who's accustomed to rubbing other people's faces in the shit.

Lomas

That's not quite true. Just because I haven't secured a good income and retired to some luxury villa –

Constance

You could kill them yourself. You could kill them, and then melt into the background, or the distance, or whatever it is professional killers melt into. You could do it. An electrical fault or a fire. No-one would realize. Why should anyone suspect? You've got no connection with me or anyone else around here. You're a total unknown.

Lomas

Even so...

Constance

Oh God – I've offended you. I'm sorry.

Lomas

Keeping her back to me, she moved across to the wooden stool, sat down, and began to compose herself. Her posture suggested a deep and well-practised piety, although her shoulders remained quite still and I was unable to discern any evidence of rosary beads or a crucifix being handled in her lap. I had the impression that she was listening intently, not to whatever might be going on in the neighbouring flat, but to me as I stood behind her; I sensed, too, that any sudden movement on my part would be met with a countervailing adjustment, a swift rotation to left or right upon the stool, so that she might continue to face away from me.

Constance

I've offended you. What can I say?

Lomas

I've no idea.

Constance

What I said was out of character. It's not like me at all, insulting a guest by making out that he's the type to have people killed.

Lomas

It makes no difference, to be honest.

Constance

I suppose it's fair to say that I've been going through a bad patch. Something's changed about the way I see everyday things. They've started assuming certain qualities, representing some-thing other than themselves, beyond themselves, and what it comes down to, usually, what they represent, it's usually death. Or if it's not death, it's the fact that I've wasted the best of my life. And I try to interpret it differently – I try to be really positive and creative – but the banality of my conclusions just makes it worse. You'd think that it'd be possible to say something good about the strangeness of everyday things, but it seems I'm incap-able of doing so; there's just death, and the fact that I've wasted the best of my life.

Lomas

Well, as I say, I'm not offended.

Constance

The other day, for instance, I found a Finnish dictionary in a skip. They'd closed this library, chucked all the stock out, and there it was, just sort of lying there, in a skip. I've never studied the Finnish language, but I've seen enough to know that it looks beautiful on the page, and so I rescued it and dusted it off and took it to the park and found a bench to sit on. And I sat there – it was unexpectedly peaceful, there was no-one around to disturb me – I just sat there, for an hour, or maybe two, just reading this dictionary. And the words, as I said, looked beautiful on the page. They seemed to represent something good at first: the prospect of moving on and starting anew, existing more fully somewhere else, cleansed of the language that had hardened all your failures and mortifications into fact, a place where all you needed to do was make the effort to speak and keep on speaking and listening, using this wonderful, alien architecture of syntax and vocabulary, and everything would be open to you – a new culture, all these new friendships and connections. I was thinking this as I browsed through the Finnish dictionary, and suddenly life seemed full of possibilities. Only it wasn't.

Lomas

No?

Constance

No. Because I'd left it too late to learn a new language from scratch. I don't care what they say; there comes a point, quite early on, when it's already far too late. The part of the brain you need, it atrophies. And closing the book, you end the stupid delusion that you can exist more fully elsewhere. Worse, you realize that it's not just that alternative way of existing that's no longer open to you; it's this one too, the life you're living now – that's closed to you too. Living like this, like I do now, it's like being in a foreign country – one where you don't speak a word of the language, or worse, where you don't even know what the language they're speaking is. That's what it's been like, the last few years. I'm ashamed to admit it, but I'm actually rather lonely.

Lomas

I tried to think of something useful to say, but all that came to mind were various platitudes I'd overheard long ago. Stuff to do with wine-tasting groups, line-dancing classes, book clubs and the like. So I said nothing.

Constance

I don't mean sex. I could have a fling, as they used to call them, whenever I wanted, if that's what I wanted. But I've got too much self-respect to go trawling the sewers. I've got high standards. The last time I went with a man, it ended up being revolting – not the sex, but what came afterwards. He seemed pleasant enough at first, and went to considerable efforts to make it pleasant for me, but in the end he just made a pig of himself, like they do. It was partly my fault, in a way. He'd already shown a bit of a tendency to boast about how filthy we'd been, congratulating himself on what I'd let him get away with, but I chose to let it pass. And then, just the once – as a kind of experiment, I suppose – I sort of joined in. I'd noticed these scabs he had on his elbows, and I was tickled, slightly thrilled by the abandon they implied, so I made some comment or other – nothing crude or explicit – just some racy little comment about the scabs and how he'd got them. And that's when he came out with this really slimy conceit, about sustaining wounds while sustaining himself on my exquisite wound. That really disgusted me. It absolutely disgusted me. He didn't see what the problem was, he insisted what he'd said was meant in fun, and when I told him he'd spoiled our time together and everything was finished, it was clear he thought I was mad. Since then, with all that's happened, it's been more difficult meeting people, especially men. I'm not interested in the fetish scene, you see. I refuse to be exploited. I refuse to be defined by my disfigurement.

Lomas

She said that with a knowing, brittle defiance, like she was challenging me to query the fact that up till then there hadn't been any obvious disfigurement on display. Her sunglasses weren't so dark that they concealed her eyes completely; the pads of skin beneath her eyes might have looked slightly puffier than they had the last time I'd seen her, but in other respects her eyes looked perfectly normal. There was her shawl, of course, and her beret, which seemed incongruous indoors; they might have been hiding something, but obviously I wasn't going to ask about what might be lurking under her clothes. Even if I remarked that I wasn't aware of any disfigurement, there was the risk that she would interpret it as a clumsy attempt to compliment her on the ownership of what might be posited as a pleasing, functional body, a body still credible as the recipient of expressions of sexual interest. I decided that the only way to proceed was to change the subject, or rather go back to an earlier one.

Constance

What I said about the dictionary must have made a certain impression, because he asked me to enlarge on the bit about moving on and starting anew and existing more fully elsewhere. When I told him I didn't have much to add to what I'd said before, he mentioned that Crump had been known to take an interest in travelling.

Lomas

Not just for weekend breaks or whatever. Actually moving away, and staying away. Did the two of you ever discuss the idea of buying a place, a smallholding, abroad?

Constance

Well, we talked about it, naturally.

Lomas

Naturally?

Constance

Lots of people were doing it back then. But it wasn't for us. There was that whole problem, you see, of shared financial commitment, which depressed him. And then of course there was the fact that all the assets were on my side and he didn't have anything of his own to bring to the table. But there was more to it than that. He might have been able to overcome whatever misgivings he had about property, sharing property as the basis for a relationship, if there'd been a chance of buying up a few acres in the Loire Valley or the Bavarian Alps or somewhere. He was actually never happier than when he was off to visit some quiet part of the countryside abroad, or rather preparing for it, brushing up on his language skills and so on, but even supposing I'd sold my house to finance a project of that sort, we'd have needed substantial amounts of cash from elsewhere to buy a suitable place, and we'd left it too late. You need to sell your soul to Mammon early on, you need to be ruthlessly strategic from the beginning — no second chances, out of your final exams and straight into the shark pool, twenty or twenty-five years making vast sums of cash by precisely those means that Crump, as a radical shirker or would-be escapee, had always resolutely dismissed.

Lomas

How about booking yourself a short break? Abroad, I mean.

Constance

Why would I want to do that?

Lomas

It would get you away from your neighbours for a while.

Constance

And how would I pay for it?

Lomas

It needn't be expensive. Or I don't suppose it would. Buy an old bike, or even rescue a bike from a skip or municipal tip, and re-condition it. Fit new cables and valve caps and brake shoes. Apply a few drops of oil where appropriate. Take your time on the back roads down, then cross the Channel as a foot passenger – if they let you take a bike on as a foot passenger. Once you're across, you don't have to spend a huge amount. You could sleep in a tent. On the continent they're fond of sleeping in tents, I under-stand. Enjoy their camping, they do, especially the French. Can't get enough of it, the French. You'd fit right in.

Constance

There'd be no point.

Lomas

I appreciate what you said about the dictionary, of course. But with a good phrasebook –

Constance

There'd be no point. Wanting to travel belongs to an earlier part of my life. It's all sealed off now, everything in it is sealed off; I can't go back.

Lomas

You're sure about that?

Constance

Perfectly sure.

Lomas

I find that going back to former interests keeps me feeling youthful.

Constance

Really?

Lomas

Really.

Constance

It's sad that I've lost it, I suppose. I used to enjoy it, planning trips away and travelling. I always took care to respect other cultures; I was very much one of those people who make a point of doing some basic research on the history and traditions of a place before they visit it. The only problem with that is, you end up perpetuating clichés – about efficiency, for example, or standards of driving, or being 'passionate', or the quality of the local food and drink. In France and Italy, I was so concerned with respecting local gastronomic cultures that I ended up making ridiculously appreciative noises over meals that were boring or tasteless or downright vile. The whole cuisine thing, I discovered, was a myth. In fact, it was so hard to buy a decent meal in France, what with the places that pretended they were food places just being closed, or selling nothing but tuna sandwiches or maybe a slice of rubbery cheese between two bits of bread, that I often resorted to dining in supermarket cafeterias, which was where I learned that the quintessential French meal is a pile of chips beneath a dollop of cheap mayonnaise. And why not? Why shouldn't they eat like that? Why live up to the stereotypes that stupid delusional foreigners want to impose on them? And what's so enviable about having a refined palate anyway? It's a monstrous indulgence, an absolute denial of what's really at stake in the process of eating. What's eating, after all, but a means of staving off death for another couple of days? I could eat porridge all day, or chips; why bother to travel hundreds of miles in search of the finest Périgord truffles? What use is a *grand cru* Saint Emilion to me now, when I could get hammered on black-market vodka and stuff my face with chips and batter and still sleep soundly on my floor for eight or nine hours?

Lomas

I see what you mean.

Constance

Was there anything else you wanted to ask me?

Lomas

I suppose not.

Constance

You'd better be off, then.

Lomas

Although she'd been calm and almost immobile throughout the exchange, I was worried that once she was alone again she'd succumb to the urge to put a glass to the wall and start listening out for sounds from next door, provoking a rapid decline in her spirits. I thought about encouraging her to abandon the flat and stay with me in my room at the department store for a week or two, but I could see that she'd be likely to interpret such a proposal as a crude attempt at seduction; I had also to consider my relationship with Juniper, whom I hadn't seen since she'd handed over the keys but who was now in effect my landlady, and whose goodwill I couldn't afford to abuse by bringing in a new and unauthorized tenant. I therefore said nothing. Constance, meanwhile, had risen from the stool and begun to shuffle backwards across the room, occasionally glancing to left or right to ensure that she continued to face away from me. When she was about three feet away, I too began to walk backwards. Reaching the main door, I turned around and tried to let myself out with a minimum of fuss, but I was defeated by the unexpectedly complex array of locks and catches securing it. Constance intervened, keeping her face to the wall as her left hand went haphazardly from one mechanism to the next. As I crossed the threshold, a loud thud from the neighbouring flat resounded through the wall.

Constance

So you'll think about it? Doing something to stop them? Not killing them, necessarily. You could just frighten them, or make lots of things go wrong for them, so they won't want to live here any more.

Lomas

I wouldn't be much good at that sort of thing. Not at the moment.

Constance

Why not?

Lomas

I've got a suspected inguinal hernia.

Constance

Well, that's it then. Clearly there's nothing more to be said.

Lomas

I tried to assure her that if anything occurred to me – anything of a practical nature, non-lethal and with a fair chance of success – I'd be in touch without delay. But as I was doing so, the door closed in my face. I left the square, and walked through the dark until I found a place that offered all-night breakfasts, and once I'd eaten I walked some more, until it was light, and then I switched on my phone and walked around in circles until I got a decent signal. I called Bettina, but she kept drifting off and referring to her tenure, the end of her tenure, and to other sorts of unpleasantness she'd been experiencing at work. She wouldn't be able to take my calls at her desk for very much longer, she said; that particular phase of our professional relationship should be considered effectively over. Never again it would be so convenient to exchange information or even chat informally; the arrangement we had was going to change forever, and for that reason she had to alert me to the business with this Vulgus character.

Bettina

He wants your notes on Crump. You know, the whole file. Not just the primary material. Not just Crump's leavings, such as they are. He wants access to your treatment of it. 'Metadata, supplementary notes, exegetical commentary.' That's how he put it.

Lomas

Sounds rather exacting.

Bettina

He was certainly in earnest.

Lomas

Aggressive with it?

Bettina

Not especially. He wants to know how you approached the investigation, how you interpreted the evidence. A précis, if you like, of the enquiry.

Lomas

Couldn't that be considered slightly intrusive?

Bettina

Well… there is such a thing as transparency.

Lomas

Does he have a first name, this Vulgus bloke? Or is Vulgus his first name?

Bettina

I suppose you'll have to find that out for yourself. When you make contact.

Lomas

You gave him my details?

Bettina

No, of course not. But I suspect he'll prove tenacious and inventive. You should be prepared.

Lomas

I didn't much care for this discussion, and when I tried to move it on to encompass other matters – my problems with the attestants, for example – I became inarticulate to a degree I hadn't experienced since the early days of my illness. At this point, Bettina became quite trenchant.

Bettina

You shouldn't conflate these people – attestants, whatever you call them – with each other. Or anyone else. It isn't healthy.

Lomas

I appreciate that. I came to the same conclusion myself, when Saoirse slipped and went sprawling on the towpath. When she attacked me that time with the tree-branch.

Bettina

Yes, but it's more than that. It's your thought processes. They're inelegant. The more you try to dissect things, the more forensic you think you're being, the more of an idiot you become. You need to stop thinking.

Lomas

How would that work?

Bettina

What I mean to say is… You need to stop trying so hard to think. It doesn't suit you. You're not a good thinker. Not in that way.

Lomas

You mean I've missed my calling in life?

Bettina

Let's be clear about this. I take it you're not coming in, I take it you're never coming in, I can tell you don't want to. And that's fine, it's probably better like that; if we saw each other now it would only be awkward. So that's what I'll leave you with — that thought, that recommendation. You need to stop trying so hard to think. You're not a good thinker. Not in that way. Goodbye, Lomas.

Lomas

Back in the department store, I relished the silence and solitude. My room was cold, but then again I wasn't disturbed by the grinding and thumping of central heating. My room was stark, but then again I could switch off the bulb altogether and lie there in the dark, enjoying the absence of visual ugliness. I slept well, and every morning I woke up refreshed. As soon as my leafleting schedule permitted, I went to the warehouse to visit Adele. She wasn't there. I tried again, a few days later, and saw that her room was slightly emptier than before. I guessed she was busy re-locating; no doubt she couldn't afford a removals firm and wanted, besides, to accomplish the move in secret, taking her possessions to the new hiding place a bagful or two at a time. Since a note might be intercepted by her mother, or the agents of her mother, I left no evidence of my visit, deciding instead to call back next day. But when I returned – three days later, as it happened, something at work cropping up in the meantime – I found the room stripped entirely bare.

Adele

That was the problem with the warehouse: too many leaks. That's why I moved back into the factory. It might have been bad, but at least the plumbing didn't explode.

Lomas

In what spare time I had, I took to hanging around outside the local clinics and food banks. Just on the off-chance.

Adele

Of course my old room wasn't an option by then; that floor had become too dangerous. Still, it suited my inclinations, where I ended up, in the boiler room. I liked it down there, I felt safe.

Lomas

In fact it occurred to me more than once that she might have gone back to live in the factory. I checked, a couple of times – just not in the boiler room. I didn't even know about the boiler room. The way down wasn't that obvious.

Adele

It made me feel less safe to know I'd been followed, that someone could see me leaving the shops or clinic or laundrette or whatever and find their way straight down to the boiler room. At least I could lock myself in, though.

Lomas

If I'd been keeping an eye on the laundrette down the road from the clinic, instead of the clinic itself, I might have saved myself an awful lot of time. But there it is. The clinic had closed for the day, so I went, and then I saw her in the distance, leaving the laundrette with a polythene sack on her back. Then it was all the way to the factory, through the yard and into the loading bay, and down. I managed to slip in just behind her. But the air was bad underground, and the light of her torch ahead was insufficient to guide me; I had a coughing fit, and tripped, and got confused, and when I finally reached the boiler room she'd gone.

Adele

Like I said, I could lock myself in. That's what I meant when I said the boiler room was safe.

Lomas

In the middle of the wall was a large and elaborate wrought-iron hatch, and in the centre of this hatch was a thick glass panel. The glass was emitting a dim yellow light that put me in mind of certain wood-burning stoves I'd seen in rural settings years before. Peering in, I saw her face, and for the first time I noticed the surgical pads secured to each side of her head. When I knocked, she waved and smiled, then bowed her head and appeared to lose herself in thought for a while. It was only when a drawer squeaked open underneath the glass panel, presenting a pencil and some paper, that I realized she'd been writing me a note. Replying in kind, I posted it back to her.

Adele

Were you followed? It's fairly safe down here but I'd rather no-one knew.

Lomas

Don't think so, no. Fancy a walk and some fresh air?

Adele

No thanks, just got some. Shopping for crackers and olives and brandy. Then to wash clothes.

Lomas

Is there a problem with your ears?

Adele

Burst eardrums. Deliberate. Unwound paperclip, stuck one end
in each ear as far as it would go.

Lomas

What for?

Adele

You know what for.

Lomas

It must have hurt a lot.

Adele

It was a logical solution to a problem, but it caused a bad infection
that hasn't cleared up yet.

Lomas

Did you get any antibiotics?

Adele

No point – they don't work, not any more. But got some pain-
killers, so I'm fine. What brings you here?

Lomas

Don't really know.

Adele

You're sure you weren't followed?

Lomas

Why would anyone want to follow me down here?

Adele

It can't be that bad or you wouldn't have come yourself. Why did you come?

Lomas

Just wanted to check.

Adele

Check what?

Lomas

Don't know. I don't recall.

Adele

Hold on. We're running out of paper.

Lomas

She posted a fresh sheet through, which I used to make an enquiry about the hatch – whether the window section opened, and if so, could she possibly open it?

Adele

What good would that do?

Lomas

Might make conversation easier.

Adele

Wouldn't for me. Can't hear means talking won't make conversation easier.

Lomas

Nevertheless, might save you paper. Half a dialogue's worth at least, since I don't say much.

Adele

I talk, you write?

Lomas

I nodded. She shrugged, and then the section of the hatch containing the window slowly creaked open. Forgetting immediately the nature of the arrangement, I started to speak, but she stopped me mid-sentence. I was taken aback, even shocked, by how loudly she spoke.

Adele

NO GOOD. YOU'LL HAVE TO WRITE IT DOWN. I'M HOPELESS AT LIP-READING.

Lomas

Is that lack of proficiency deliberate?

Adele

VERY PERCEPTIVE. YOU'RE A VERY PERCEPTIVE MAN.

Lomas

How have you been?

Adele

DO YOU MIND IF WE CHANGE THE SUBJECT?

Lomas

What shall we talk about instead?

Adele

DON'T KNOW. I NEVER KNOW, BUT THAT HARDLY MATTERS NOW. I DON'T HAVE TO THINK ABOUT IT, TALKING, NOT ANY MORE.

Lomas

I tried to find you at the warehouse.

Adele

IT GOT HORRIBLE THERE, UNLIVEABLE. IT WENT RANK – BECAUSE OF THE LEAKS. I DIDN'T NEED THE EXTRA STRESS; I WAS GETTING ENOUGH OF THAT AT WORK.

Lomas

I didn't realize you were working.

Adele

WHAT ELSE WOULD I LIVE ON? I HAD CASUAL WORK CUTTING FLOWERS, CARNATIONS MAINLY, FOR DISTRIBUTION TO A CHAIN OF FLORIST OUTLETS, CASH IN HAND. IT WAS RUN BY A GANG OF CRIMINALS, BUT I COULDN'T AFFORD TO BE CHOOSY, AND AT SOME POINT SOMEONE SAID I HAD A NICE TELEPHONE VOICE, SO NEXT THING I KNEW I WAS WORKING IN THIS OFFICE MADE OF CORRUGATED METAL, ONE OF THOSE BOXES THEY USE ON BUILDING SITES, LIKE PORTABLE TOILETS BUT BIGGER. THEN ANOTHER GANG BOUGHT THE FIRST GANG OUT AND STARTED TO MAKE THE BUSINESS MORE LEGITIMATE SO THEY COULD USE IT FOR LAUNDERING MONEY. THAT MEANT SUDDENLY I WAS ON AN OFFICIAL PAYROLL AND THEY WANTED MY ADDRESS. I DECIDED TO GET A PROPER JOB THEN, AND MAYBE PUT THE WRONG ADDRESS ON THE FORMS OR SIMPLY CHANGE MY ADDRESS MORE OFTEN. AND THAT'S WHAT I DID, I GOT A NEW JOB, A JOB IN AN OFFICE. IT WAS A NOISY OFFICE, THE BUSINESS HAD SOMETHING TO DO WITH SELLING THE PERSONAL DETAILS OF PRIVATE INDIVIDUALS ON TO COMPANIES WHOSE BUSINESS IT WAS TO SELL THINGS NO-ONE REALLY WANTED TO BUY. OR MAYBE

THEY DID WANT TO BUY THEM; PEOPLE TEND TO CONVINCE THEMSELVES THEY NEED ALL SORTS OF RUBBISH, DON'T YOU FIND?

Lomas

That's right.

Adele

IN MY PREVIOUS JOB THE ONLY OTHER PERSON IN THE OFFICE WAS SOME GANGSTER'S MOLL, OR MAYBE SHE WAS HIS MOTHER. I WASN'T EXACTLY SURE HOW OLD SHE WAS. MOST OF THE TIME IT WAS FINE; SHE JUST SAT THERE FIDDLING WITH HER MAKEUP AND HER PHONE. THE ONLY PROBLEM WAS SHE SOMETIMES USED MY DESK, AND THEN THERE'D BE SLIME FROM HER FACE ALL OVER THE TELEPHONE HANDSET, OR THERE'D BE GREASE FROM HER HANDS ALL OVER MY PENS AND PENCILS; THERE'D BE FOOD DEBRIS ALL OVER THE PLACE, AND STICKY CIRCLES FROM CUPS ALL OVER MY PAPERWORK. BUT MOSTLY IT WAS FINE, AS I SAY, AND AT LEAST WE HAD NOTHING IN COMMON, SO THERE WASN'T THAT MUCH TO TALK ABOUT. IN THE NEW PLACE, THOUGH, IT WAS DIFFERENT. IN THE NEW PLACE IT WAS REVOLTING. ONE OF MY COLLEAGUES HAD A COMPULSIVE URGE TO DISCUSS HER BODY AND ALL THE VARIOUS NOISES IT MADE IN THE PROCESS OF ITS OWN MAINTENANCE. SO WHENEVER SHE YAWNED SHE HAD TO TELL YOU EXACTLY WHY SHE WAS YAWNING, AND WHEN SHE SNEEZED SHE HAD TO TELL YOU WHY SHE WAS SNEEZING, AND WHEN HER STOMACH RUMBLED SHE'D HAVE TO EXPLAIN ABOUT THAT. I COULD ACCEPT WITHIN CERTAIN LIMITS THE SOUND OF HER VOICE, AND I COULD ACCEPT WITHIN CERTAIN LIMITS THE SOUNDS OF HER BODY WITH ITS INTERIOR VOIDS AND

BLOCKAGES, BUT WHEN SHE TALKED ABOUT THE SOUNDS HER BODY WAS MAKING SHE REDUCED HERSELF TO THE STATUS OF AN AUTOMATON; WHAT IMPRESSED YOU MORE THAN ANYTHING WAS THE GHASTLY CIRCULARITY OF THIS CLOSED AND SELF-PERPETUATING SYSTEM IN WHICH A MOUTH GENERATED PROGRESS REPORTS ON A BODY THAT KEPT A MOUTH IN THE BUSINESS OF GENERATING PROGRESS REPORTS ON A BODY. EVEN THEN, THE SYSTEM COULDN'T BE SAID TO BE CLOSED, NOT TRULY CLOSED, BECAUSE IT WAS RAVENOUS, LEAVING NOTHING FOR ANYONE ELSE, NO SPACE, NO SILENCE, IT WAS DISGUSTING AND SHE DIDN'T EVEN REALIZE, AND IF SHE'D REALIZED SHE WOULDN'T HAVE CARED, SHE WANTED MORE BABIES, AND THE OTHERS WERE JUST AS BAD WHEN IT CAME TO BABIES, THEY WERE OBSESSED WITH HAVING MORE BABIES, THAT'S ALL THEY TALKED ABOUT, THE NEED TO CREATE NEW MOUTHS, TO FORCE NEW MOUTHS OUT FROM THEIR VAGINAS, WHICH WAS THE ONLY REALLY TRANSCENDENT MORAL VIRTUE, PRODUCING MORE RAVENOUS BODIES WITH JABBERING MOUTHS ATTACHED, MORE MOUTHS ON BODIES PILING UP IN EVERY DIRECTION, TO EVERY HORIZON, DEMANDING MORE HOUSES, MORE CARS, MORE CHILDREN, NOISIER HOLIDAYS, BIGGER PENISES, THICKER PENISES, BETTER ORGASMS, NOISIER ORGASMS, DAYS IN THE SUN, MORE NOISE, MORE SLIME AND TIGHTER VAGINAS, MORE SYMMETRICAL, THE SPATTERING SPURTING FURTHER, LEAVING NO SPACE NO SILENCE ANYWHERE.

Lomas

Yes, that's right. I know the type.

Adele

HIDING IN THE TOILET WAS NO GOOD. THEY'D FOL-
LOW ME IN AND KEEP ON TALKING WHILE PERFORM-
ING THEIR BODILY FUNCTIONS. I TRIED TO THINK OF A
WAY TO ESCAPE AND REMEMBERED HOW I USED TO
IMMERSE MYSELF IN WATER, IN THE SEA, WHENEVER I
COULD, BECAUSE WITH MY HEAD SUBMERGED I
COULDN'T HEAR THE NOISE. BUT YOU CAN'T KEEP
YOUR HEAD UNDERWATER FOREVER; YOU DROWN,
OR PEOPLE COME ALONG AND START THRASHING
ABOUT AND PULLING THEIR TRUNKS OR BIKINI BOT-
TOMS DOWN, OR CHILDREN COME ALONG AND JUMP
IN THE WATER AND YOU GET URINE IN YOUR MOUTH
OR MAYBE SOME FAECES WILL FLOAT PAST. BURSTING
MY EARDRUMS WITH A SHARP BIT OF WIRE WAS THE
ONLY REALISTIC ALTERNATIVE. THAT LEFT ME UN-
QUALIFIED FOR TELEPHONE WORK OF COURSE, AND I
LOST MY JOB BECAUSE THEY KNEW IT WAS SELF-
INFLICTED. IN ANY CASE, NO-ONE FELT COMFORT-
ABLE WORKING IN THE SAME OFFICE AS ME; THEY
THOUGHT I WAS DISTURBED AND NEEDED COUNSEL-
LING OR ELECTROCONVULSIVE SHOCK THERAPY OR
WHATEVER. NEXT I TRIED TO GET A JOB DELIVERING
PAPERS; I LIKED THE IDEA OF BEING OUT AND ABOUT,
BUT MAINLY THEY WANTED YOUTHS FOR THAT KIND
OF WORK, AND SO WHEN I ASKED AROUND THE
NEWSAGENTS THEY ALL THOUGHT I WAS MOCKING
THEM, TAKING THE PISS, AND NO-ONE WOULD HIRE
ME.

Lomas

Yes, they're like gold dust, jobs delivering things from a sack.

Adele

I'M DOING CLEANING WORK NOW. DISPOSAL OF MED-

ICAL WASTE FOR A PRIVATE CONTRACTOR.

Lomas

With gloves?

Adele

I HAVE TO SUPPLY MY OWN.

Lomas

It's not what it used to be, casual work.

Adele

STRANGE HOW SO MUCH HORROR SHOULD ORIGI-
NATE IN SUCH A TINY PLACE. FAR SMALLER THAN THE
INTESTINES, FOR EXAMPLE.

Lomas

What – the mouth, the rumbling stomach, or the womb?

Adele

NO, WHAT I MEAN IS, HAVE YOU EVER PLACED ONE
HAND ON TOP OF YOUR HEAD AND PUSHED YOUR
TONGUE UP AGAINST THE ROOF OF YOUR MOUTH
AND PAUSED TO CONSIDER HOW LITTLE SPACE LIES
BETWEEN THEM? AND HOW EVERYTHING YOU'VE
EVER KNOWN AND WILL EVER KNOW IS CONTAINED
IN THAT TINY SPACE BETWEEN YOUR TONGUE AND
THE PALM OF YOUR HAND? I WAS DOING THAT ONE
DAY WHEN I FELT A LUMP ON THE ROOF OF MY
MOUTH. NATURALLY I WAS AFRAID. I THOUGHT IT
WAS CANCER.

Lomas

And was it?

Adele

NO, IT WAS JUST A LUMP ON THE ROOF OF MY MOUTH.

Lomas

I need some fresh air. Do you want to come with me up to the surface?

Adele

NOT TODAY. LIKE I SAID, I'VE BEEN OUT ONCE AL-READY. BESIDES, I'VE GOT JOBS TO DO.

Lomas

Bring them with you.

Adele

I CAN'T, THEY'RE CHORES. SORTING LAUNDRY, TIDY-ING UP, THAT SORT OF THING.

Lomas

May I leave you my details?

Adele

WHAT SORT OF DETAILS?

Lomas

Contact details. You might need to contact me at some point.

Adele

I CAN'T HOLD A TELEPHONE CONVERSATION.

Lomas

You could leave a message.

Adele

CONCERNING WHAT?

Lomas

I don't know. An emergency.

Adele

YOU EXPECT ME TO HAVE AN EMERGENCY?

Lomas

I'm just saying. I'm thinking ahead.

Adele

AHEAD TO WHAT? WHAT'S GOING TO HAPPEN TO ME? AND WHY SHOULD YOU BE BURDENED WITH MY PROBLEMS? WHAT COULD YOU DO ABOUT THEM ANY-WAY?

Lomas

I've got the temporary use of a room. A comfortable office, with a choice of sofa or desktop to sleep on, a sink in the corner, a light switch that works and a light bulb that works, and no-one ever around except the owner, who never comes in.

Adele

ALL RIGHT, LEAVE YOUR NUMBER. I'LL COPY IT LATER INTO THE BOOK.

Lomas

Back in the factory yard, I gulped cold air and hawked up phlegm. My mouth and throat and lungs felt polluted; I needed some whisky or something to fumigate my tubes. I found an outdoor tap, and washed my face and hands. Then I went looking for a shop that sold strong drink.

9

Lomas

Juniper eventually secured a suitable buyer for the department store, as I learned one afternoon from a letter requesting I leave my keys in the upstairs office for collection by the end of the following week. Although essentially a notice of eviction, the letter was cordial; a postscript invited me to call in at the flat if I had anything to report on the current whereabouts of Crump.

In fact I wasn't sorry to leave, as my last few nights had been disturbed by sounds of dripping, and in the mornings there'd been puddles on the floor. On the night of the eviction notice, the dripping sounds had been joined by a frantic scratching, and sometimes a tapping, somewhere deep in the walls or behind them. It sounded rather like a domestic pet impatient for food or exercise, or a bird trapped behind a fireplace, and it made me think of Saoirse. The sense of resentment and disgust, the putative aptitude for hatred, the scratching and gouging during the wrestling match on the floor, and now a claw-tipped, bestial scrabbling in the walls. It made me uneasy.

I'd bought a second-hand bike by this point, a stately old roadster which had been modified to the extent that you could describe it as a tricycle of sorts. Equipped with a sidecar that was capacious enough to accommodate my possessions, it wasn't quick, but as a vehicle for touring it was ideal. As I creaked away from the loading bay, I felt an unexpectedly convincing sense of purpose.

In roadside hostels, I heard Saoirse as mammal or bird, the scrabbling claw-strokes, the scuttering wing-bones, in the skirting boards and ceilings.

In my tent, I heard her scratching away at the flysheet, but when I ventured out to investigate I found no-one, human or otherwise, not so much as a bat or a moth.

I called Bettina, but the first few times the phone just rang out and no-one bothered to answer, and the next few times I got the voice of some bloke who insisted on telling me his first name and wanted to know how he could assist me with my valued enquiry today. Eventually the number wasn't recognized at all, so I gave up.

Because I was running out of pretexts for further visits to the attestants and urgently needed to perpetuate the illusion that my research was making progress, I'd acted on Juniper's rather heavy-handed hints about Crump's male friends. The file suggested that they were drawn almost exclusively from his youth – to be precise, his time at secondary school. If he'd failed to establish lasting male friendships thereafter – at university, during his forays into politics and, yet later, in the workplace – the reasons behind it weren't really hinted at by the documents in hand.

Crump [box file]

Ludo and I had queued for several hours to see the eminent philosopher give his last ever public lecture. He'd emerged from semi-retirement to deliver what had been billed as a summation of his life's work, and though that work was no longer fashionable, with even some of his closest adherents privately admitting that his arguments in favour of the global codification of the rights of non-sentient properties were methodologically flawed, his reputation was such that the hall in which the event was being held was full to capacity. Even I, whose admiration for his work was somewhat tempered, owing more to broad ideological sympathy than any close identification with the substance of the canon, felt the excitement in the hall; there was a sense of civic occasion which transcended the narrow academic origins of the affair. As for Ludo – twenty, energetic and earnest, deeply committed to the cause – he was like a kid at a rock concert. When the philosopher shuffled onstage and the applause began, he turned to me, Ludo, clapping like the rest but with the craziest of grins: 'It's the greatest living philosopher!' All was not well, though. Lines were fluffed; the old man kept losing his place and struggling to find his way back to it; then, opening up the lecture to the floor and taking a carefully worded challenge from some pompous young buck determined to make an impression, he frankly confessed to not understanding the question at all – provoking scattered uncomfortable laughter and some sympathetic applause. Only years later, when I read the old fellow's obituary, did I realize that he'd probably been exhibiting the early signs of the slow cerebral atrophy that would ultimately kill him. And the lecture? No-one involved, it seemed to me, came out of that hall with very much credit. Ludo included. Me included. It still makes me cringe.

Lomas

What seemed clear was that the school group had been fairly close – close enough, at least, to survive the friends' extensive migrations over the decades. Even now, they met once a year for what I gathered was a kind of collective regression: hiring a holiday cottage and spending a long weekend there, drinking to excess, talking bullshit, raising a glass to the absent Crump. The file said nothing about these annual reunions; it was by contacting one of the friends, a senior tax consultant called Victor, whose correspondence made an appearance in the file, that I was informed of the tradition. We agreed to meet in the course of the next reunion, which was scheduled five weeks hence. The venue: a lay-by on a single-carriageway A road, close to a pub that one of the friends was keen to visit.

At the appointed time I was there, astride my tricycle. Five minutes later, a four-wheel-drive pulled in. Four middle-aged passengers stared out blearily; only the driver seemed alert to his surroundings. He lowered the windows, turned the engine off, and got out. The others remained inside the cabin.

Victor

Mr... Lomas?

Lomas

I told him just Lomas would do, he said that he was Vic, and after introducing the others he asked me what I'd managed to turn up on Crump so far. I equivocated slightly, working the question round to what the group believed had been responsible for driving Crump away, and what they knew about the attestants.

Victor

We didn't talk about that kind of thing, to be perfectly honest.

Lomas

That kind of thing?

Victor

You know. Relationships.

James

The ladies. Personal problems.

Eric

So what *do* we talk about, James?

James

Please ignore Eric. He's off his pips with hash and light ales. You're not to trust him.

Victor

Lomas knows what we talk about – broadly, up to a point. I've already told him.

Eric

What did you tell him?

Victor

That we sit around and talk bullshit.

Eric

Such as?

Victor

I don't know. I suppose you just have to be there.

Tim

So… we bullshit?

James

Absolutely. On our great fat hairy arses. Sit and bullshit.

Lomas

Whatever tension there was in the vehicle – and it was there, like the fug of stale alcohol and overheated crevices that seeped from the open windows – it preceded their arrival in the lay-by. Maybe the pub had been a terrible disappointment, or maybe they'd disagreed over the level of air-conditioning in the car, or maybe the air-con had failed altogether and they were simply hot and tired. I wondered if every year turned out like this.

Gareth

What about you, Lomas? You got funny stories to tell – about Crump, for example?

Lomas

I don't think so. No – not funny ones.

Gareth

You interested in… what was it… moral philosophy? Just like he was?

Lomas

Not like he was.

Gareth

You do any plumbing, DIY, anything like that?

Lomas

I'm afraid not. Those are decent skills to have, I know, but I'm not sure I'd really get the chance to use them, if I had them. Or not very often – the way things are.

Eric

Any hobbies or pastimes?

Lomas

Really just language acquisition. Yes, I'm trying to develop my foreign language skills.

Gareth

It's just like Crump was here among us! Foreign languages! Bikes! The spirit of Crump lives on!

Victor

Have a care, Gareth. We don't even know for certain he's dead.

Lomas

There was a short, uncomfortable silence. Eric got out of the car and dabbed his dripping forehead with the hem of his logoed T-shirt, exposing his gut and provoking a swift comedic insult from Gareth or Tim; I didn't catch which one it was. The other three followed, milling around outside the vehicle. The tall one, James, kneeled down and began to inspect the drivetrain of my tricycle.

Eric

So, Lomas. What first aroused your interest in Crump?

Lomas

Oh, the usual. His insights into the nature of human existence. That kind of thing.

Gareth

How did you know? About the insights, I mean. Into the nature of human existence.

Lomas

A colleague told me.

Gareth

Which colleague?

Lomas

One who used to work with me before my extended sabbatical began.

Gareth

What was his name?

Lomas

The colleague? Bettina. She was a woman. Called Bettina.

Gareth

I don't know her. Anyone know her?

Lomas

The other four shook their heads and mumbled. None of them knew her.

Victor

What does it matter? The insights were hardly much of a secret. I've no idea what they were, the insights, but Crump, I know, was famous for having had them. I suppose that's how she heard, this former colleague of yours – Bettina, you said? Because of his reputation.

Lomas

What was it based on, his reputation?

Victor

Oh, all sorts of things. His parables, for example. Little stories, often quite humorous ones, about dreams he'd had, or whatever.

James

You should tell him the story of Crump and the sorrowful self-as-a-child.

Eric

Yes, go on – tell Lomas the story of Crump and the sorrowful self-as-a-child.

Victor

Well, from what I can remember, it's like this. Crump had this dream in which his self-as-a-child was taking him on a tour of his childhood haunts. And so his self-as-a-child, it pointed out his old school, the fields he'd played in, the lanes he'd raced along on his bike, all places like that. And Crump kept asking it, the self-as-a-child, what conclusions he should draw from what it was showing him. Eventually his self-as-a-child looked up at him, and it told him he'd wasted his life. 'You've wasted your life,' it said. And that's the story of Crump and the sorrowful self-as-a-child.

Tim

Honestly, that story, it was priceless. And it meant we got the chance to make all these brilliant jokes about how he needed to see some kind of professional who'd be able to help him figure out what the dream was about and what it was trying to tell him.

James

It was quite funny, at the time. He found it funny. That's why he told us. He thought it was funny.

Victor

The problem was, the parable gained a wider currency, and things got out of hand. Admiration for it soon became so general that it got into the public domain, and news of it finally reached his parents. They were genuinely upset to learn that he felt he'd wasted his life.

Lomas

Is that why he needed to get away? Because the joke had got out of hand?

Victor

Well, no, the getting away came later. That was all a bit mysterious. No-one knew what lay behind it.

Lomas

He didn't articulate the reasons in a parable?

Victor

No. The older he got, the less he had to say for himself.

James

I think we're ready to go. I'm out of booze.

Lomas

Everyone, even Victor, now seemed weary and out of sorts. I thanked the five of them for their time and cycled off.

10

Lomas

I didn't feel up to a further interview with Juniper just yet, and was convinced that my priorities lay elsewhere. She was doing pretty well for herself, after all; she'd managed to liquidize her assets and had probably paid off the mortgage on her flat. I hadn't believed her when she'd claimed there'd be no money left over to spend on other projects; I imagined her enjoying a three-month cruise, or looking around for a rural property to restore in Haute-Garonne. She'd bought her way out of a grubby situation which, it seemed to me, all five of us and Crump had formerly shared – a situation largely impervious to the blandishments of her pseudo-pantheistic system of values, or however you wanted to categorize that tissue of platitudes ripped off from cheesy self-help books. That spasm of self-loathing towards the end of her account of the inheritance might have been touching in its directness, but it seemed to leave no doubt that she anticipated no other course in life than that dictated by money. From which it followed that, in the short term – or at least until her cash ran out – my place was with the others, in so far as I had a place, for I had no place.

Cycling during the quiet hours just after dawn, retreating behind the roadside hedges when the traffic got too heavy, and feeding on cheap white bread and tinned sardines when hungry, I made my way back to the block of flats where Saoirse lived, or where Saoirse had lived, not really expecting to find her at home any more. I'd been tormented at every stopover by the scrabbling of the claw-strokes and the scuttering of the wing-bones, which were so frantic now that they seemed to speak of some personal catastrophe, such as the termination of Saoirse's tenancy agreement. And my pessimism was justified: when I arrived, I found that her building had been demolished. Trenches brimmed with yellow water, fluorescent tabards moved obscurely among the ruins, the odd expletive could be heard, a frail-looking man in a stained cagoule was watching blankly from the perimeter, a small dog waterproofed in tartan was shivering miserably at his feet, the tartan was stained but not as badly as the cagoule, and who was I to assess the dirtiness of other sentient beings, who to comparativize the stains of dogs and men? What had used me as a toilet among the hedgerows I dared not think; I didn't know the relevant Latin, hadn't acquired it, hadn't got round to buying the field book, and in any case I'd been sleeping, sleeping fitfully, when the faecal deeds had been done. And I was still troubled by the ethical implications of my last meeting with Adele. I couldn't think what to make of it, what to infer from it, how to proceed from it in an appropriately constructive and sensitive way. Which left only Constance.

In the square, the broken glass was as bad as before. I had to wheel my tricycle deftly, not wanting to squander the last few patches in my repair kit. Constance didn't exactly refuse to let me in; she didn't have to, I didn't ask. What right had I to be admitted, what case could I make? None whatsoever.

We talked through the letterbox. When she spoke, I saw her mouth. When she listened, I saw one ear and also one eye. The dark heavy spectacles had gone.

Constance

I sometimes wondered why he kept on coming back, apart from his interest in the Crump thing, which in any case seemed to feature less and less in our discussions. If he was fond of me in his own weird way, he certainly never let on. But there was this sense I had, an odd impression of… I don't know… as though he was keeping an eye on me, or looking out for my welfare in a hopeless kind of way. It got a bit onerous. That last time, I was possibly rather harsh on him. I gave him pretty short shrift. But I was getting out and about by then, despite my mobility problems

– making an effort with my social life and even meeting men again; I didn't want him messing all that up for me, bringing me down. It would have been nice if we'd parted more amicably, of course, but there you go. I think he just caught me on a bad day.

Lomas

You may remember my suggestion that you take a short break. A getaway break. A holiday abroad. You weren't impressed by it, I recall.

Constance

What are you talking about?

Lomas

My suggestion. You weren't taken with it.

Constance

A getaway break?

Lomas

In France or somewhere. Italy, Spain, even Switzerland. Or Austria. It depends on which of the languages you prefer. Unless you choose to base the decision on ease of access, in which case France is probably best. You may remember I mentioned camping.

Constance

You're inviting me to go camping?

Lomas

No. Unless you actually want to. If you wanted to, I'd be happy to place my gear at your disposal. But that wasn't my intention. If you remember, I suggested you go camping in France or somewhere as a means of getting away from your domestic situation. But I don't want to broadcast it here on the doorstep, where politically sensitive details might be overheard.

Constance

You want me to let you into the building.

Lomas

No. I wouldn't be so contriving. I'm not inviting you to go camping and I'm not attempting to worm my way by subterfuge into the building. It's just that last time, when you mentioned the expense involved, before you said what you said about there being no point in going at all, I made some remarks about how you could do up a bike and travel abroad quite cheaply. I think I said that you could get one from a tip. But if you don't like raking through tips, you could go to a shop, a specialist shop, a shop that specializes in reconditioned bikes. That's why I came. I've got a reconditioned bike that I bought from a shop; I got it quite cheaply, though it's really more of a tricycle. That's to say it's got a sidecar attached, a pod with a wheel, and a space for stowing your luggage. I came to show you.

Constance

Thanks, but I can't ride a bike any more. Not without certain modifications.

Lomas

If it's arthritis, something like that —

Constance

No, it's worse than that. My foot's off.

Lomas

Sorry?

Constance

My foot. It had to come off. For medical reasons.

Lomas

I had no idea.

Constance

Why should you?

Lomas

No reason at all. I'm sorry.

Constance

I'd been having problems for ages. It was just one thing after another, in terms of my health. I had a tumour in my stomach, for example. It wasn't malignant, but it had to be removed. So I went in and had it cut out. And it was huge. They showed me afterwards. It even had a face. Tumours do, you know; it's quite common. And my tumour's face was supplicating; its expression was like something you'd see on the face of a martyr in some Baroque religious painting.

Lomas

Yes – I know the expression you mean.

Constance

Incidentally – just so you know – there wasn't any kind of mystical significance in the phenomenon, not for me. It was simply a tumour. They took it away, and that was that, or so I thought. But then it grew back. And the second time it didn't have a face; it was just an ordinary tumour. They took it away. Let that be an end to it, I thought. But it wasn't the end; it kept growing back. And my stomach, or more accurately my midriff, which I'd worked so hard to keep flat and toned and free from unsightly flab, turned into a mass of unsightly scar tissue, all kind of lumpy and crisscrossed with lines. With everything else that went on, my midriff should have been the least of my worries, but there you go; it's funny, the stuff you get obsessed about when things aren't going so well.

Lomas

I wondered what the aetiological link, if any, might be between the tumours and the amputated foot, and whether she wanted me to ask. It might be the right thing to do, to ask, but there seemed little to be gained from it; besides, her earlier guardedness suggested that such questions would not be welcome. You never knew with people; you never knew what they wanted from you, especially when some confidence was at stake.

Through the letterbox I could see her mouth, which was closed, or almost closed; and then, for a longer moment, her eyes, which were slightly unfocused. At last she blinked. The flap on her side of the door snapped shut. I lowered the flap on my side. Then I retreated.

Next time I saw her, she was picking her way between bins in the filthy alleyway, holding the skirts of her cloak in one hand to keep the hems from dragging through excrement and ordure, the tip of her walking stick probing assuredly as she hobbled. The visual contrast between the heavy black corduroy cloak and her bright pink training shoes was striking, but not in a good way; it made me feel sorry for her, and I felt she'd taken a risk in leaving the flat and crossing the square in view of her persecutors like that, so imperfectly gothic and melodramatic in her dress. Just as well she had the walking stick, which seemed to explain away, at least to a certain extent, her obvious lack of belonging. Here's that eccentric spinster-divorcee, the stick proclaimed; she has the right (a limited right) to be eccentric, her leg doesn't work, she has a medical case for clemency. Or something like that; I might have been wrong; it was just a feeling I had as I watched her. And I reminded myself that walking sticks were again coming into fashion among the hiking fraternity — I'd noticed that on my travels — so maybe it wasn't quite as powerful a totem as I'd imagined.

She walked too slowly for me to follow on the bike, or rather the trike, and so I pushed the bike or trike along the pavement, keeping my distance, until we came to our destination: a greasy spoon with gourmet pretensions, trading in fry-ups, thick-cut chips and luxury ketchups. Constance entered; through the window I saw her taking her place at a table with a man. I chained the tricycle to some railings round the back and counted my money. I was hungry and needed a drink; as long as I didn't leave a tip, my funds should just about stretch to a one-course meal and some beer. Since most of the tables were unoccupied, I didn't have too much trouble persuading reception to admit me, despite the fact that I'd brought in my luggage, all three bags of it, from the sidecar. Declining the shadowy corner offered to me, I made my way to a table not far from Constance and the man, where I ordered two fried eggs with chips, a slice of bread and butter, and a strong *bière belge blonde*. Once the waitress had departed, I learned that Constance and her companion were planning an evening of passion together.

Man

First I'll be wanting to look at your boobs – including the nipples.

Constance

We'll need to sort out that light in the lounge. It hasn't been working for a while now. Not for three days.

Man

We could light some candles.

Constance

That's not a permanent solution.

Man

It'll be romantic. You'll see. You'll like it. And once I've looked at your boobs, including the nipples, and had a quick feel and a lick of them, I'll be wanting to pull your knickers down. That'd be great.

Constance

I tried a new bulb, a brand-new bulb, one with a slightly lower wattage. It made no difference.

Man

Two or three candles should be enough to light your privates up. Or maybe we'll use a torch. I'll look at your front parts in some detail, then I'll turn you round and have a look at your bum, if that's OK.

Constance

It might be the wiring or something like that. Are you any good with electrics?

Lomas

It got to the point where I couldn't hear what they were saying; the place had started to fill up with newcomers, and they were rowdy types, shouting and swearing and making lewd remarks as they tried to find somewhere to sit. All but a few were dressed in football shirts or rugby jerseys – I couldn't tell the difference – and some of the males appeared to be sparring with each other while their companions, grinning and cheering, filmed the proceedings. I got down on the floor and carefully rolled my salt cellar in the direction of Constance's table, hoping to hear more once I got closer. It was then that I discovered that most of the newcomers were naked from the waist downwards.

There'd been nothing in the signage outside to indicate that the restaurant might be of a specialist nature. In my experience, greasy spoons with gourmet pretentions didn't usually cater to nudism or free love. Then again, it had been a long time since I'd dined in a formal setting, and I knew that cultural mores could change quickly. Constance, at least, was still tightly buttoned up in her cloak, with nothing on show. In her hands was a latex mask, produced in the likeness of a zombie or other putrefying undead, which she was unrolling like a condom over the head of her dining companion. As she did so, he continued to make unpleasantly puerile remarks about his plans for her later that evening. She briefly silenced him by pushing the band of latex over his mouth, but once the lips were in place he wiggled his tongue through the slit and started again. Glancing away, she noticed me crouching on the floor. She looked first mortified, then annoyed; after a moment she made an impatient, brushing gesture, as to dismiss me.

I picked up the salt cellar and, with a minimum of direct contact, made my way back through the crowd towards my own table. Barring my way after several yards were a man and a woman. Lips peeled back, they were lunging extravagantly at each other and then recoiling, their snarling grins expressing something like mutual triumph. I felt vaguely humbled, in the way that one might feel humbled when viewing large predators at close quarters in a zoo, but soon recovered; after all, the couple had nothing to do with me, I had no wish to lunge extravagantly and recoil, and I saw no merit in equating oneself, or seeking to equate oneself, in status, psychological or otherwise, with large predators in zoos. I edged around them and pushed on through.

My meal was waiting for me at my table, but it had been ruined; someone had used it as the basis for a sex act, reducing the two fried eggs to a smear and the pile of chips to a gold-streaked bed of mashed potato in which the imprint of two buttocks and an anus was just about visible. On the positive side, my beer was still in its bottle. But I was cross about the chips, which I regarded as my fuel for the journey to come. I didn't see why, if the owners couldn't be bothered to keep an orderly house, I should be made to pay for food I hadn't consumed. So I just sat and sipped my beer until I saw Constance and the man preparing to go, at which point I gathered my luggage together and slunk off behind them, leaving a handful of coins by the plate – a rather insulting amount, a quarter of the price of one *bière blonde*.

I took my time, I didn't want to intrude on their love-games, didn't want to see them lunging or recoiling or whatever they planned to do in the course of the evening, and I thought that by calling in at a shop for some beer on the way and then waiting for half an hour on the edge of the square I'd be giving them ample opportunity to get it all over and done with, but I miscalculated; actually they hadn't even got started when I turned up at the flat, where Constance wasn't pleased to see me.

Constance

You shouldn't have come. Why did you come?

Lomas

The spatial proportions of the lounge had been much reduced since my previous visit. In one corner, angled upwards on an old shoebox, was a small electric torch whose meagre glow revealed that the walls had encroached by two or three feet on each side while the ceiling was now just a couple of inches above my head. The dado rails to which Constance had devoted such painstaking attention were no longer to be seen. The window had been blocked off, and the main light fitting, which had previously hung from a cord, was now embedded in the ceiling.

Constance

I saw you at the restaurant. I could tell you were listening in. It's really not on, you know. It's really not on at all.

Lomas

Sorry. What happened at the restaurant made me think that coming here would be the honourable thing to do. In the circum-stances, I mean.

Constance

How the hell do you work that out?

Lomas

I placed you in a compromising position.

Constance

Oh, you think?

Lomas

And I believed that I was culpable. In the circumstances, I mean.

Constance

Why do you keep saying that? What circumstances?

Lomas

To be honest, I don't know. It's just empty rhetoric. Not even rhetoric. Just a platitude. Something to say.

Constance

God give me strength.

Lomas

Yes, I've been wondering about that. I kept meaning to ask. Are you religious at all? Some aspects of your posture on a previous occasion suggested rosary beads, I thought.

Constance

This is becoming tedious.

Lomas

I know.

Constance

The odd thing is, I actually liked you for a while. At least, I didn't actively dislike you; I thought you seemed quite nice. A decent bloke. Now I can see you're nothing but a nuisance.

Lomas

Where's your man?

Constance

On the toilet. We had to leave straight after the starter. He's got a bit of an upset tummy.

Lomas

Will he still have the mask on?

Constance

When he comes out? Yes, I expect so.

Lomas

And you're happy to have him here, in the flat, as your guest?

Constance

What do you think?

Lomas

Don't ask me. I don't know anything.

Constance

What would you do about it, his being here, if I wasn't? Happy, I mean.

Lomas

Don't know that either. By the way, what's up with your lounge?

Constance

The light doesn't work. I did try changing the bulb. You probably overheard me saying before. I put a new one in, a new one with a slightly lower wattage. It made no difference.

Lomas

I meant the size.

Constance

Oh, that. It's soundproofing. Or it would have been, if it had worked. I couldn't afford to get a company that specialized in acoustic surveying and soundproofing, so I got this man I'd heard of down at the clinic to take a look. A cheap odd-job man. He said he could do the job at a fraction of the price of a specialist company; it wouldn't be perfect in terms of fit and finish et cetera but it would work, it would be effective. So I booked him and he came. And this is what happened. He botched it completely. He ripped me off. He didn't even use proper materials, he just carted in a load of cardboard and mattresses, sacks of office waste, all sorts of old rubbish, carpets, egg boxes, polystyrene and the like. He called it 'low-impact acoustic insulation' and he packed it against the walls. Oh yes, and the ceiling. And then he boarded it all up, and none too thoroughly at that. The last few panels kept falling off; I had to keep nailing them back in myself. I never heard from him again. He disappeared, as rogue tradesmen do. And I can still hear the people next door – playing loud music and having loud sex and making nasty personal comments about my appearance.

Lomas

It can be risky, I've heard, getting tradesmen in for unconventional jobs.

Constance

I should really strip it all out and restore the original dimensions of the room, but I've got a suspicion that he packed in a load of asbestos panels and tiles with the rest of the rubbish. And it's not just the lounge; I paid him to soundproof the bedroom as well. So now it's too small for a double bed. Not that I own a double bed. These days I tend to sleep on the floor; I find it's better for my back. Come on, I'll show you.

Lomas

Her bedroom was tiny, like a walk-in cupboard or cell. The fit of the panels that held the insulation in place was almost comically bad, with some of the gaps between them sealed with gaffer tape, others pumped with caulk which had dried to a bulging crust. In one corner of the room, an off-white panel had been tentatively stained with the smeary pink dye I recalled from the dado rail in the lounge.

Spread out on the floor was a frayed tarpaulin. On the tarpaulin lay a thin and faded pallet, a pillow, a folded sheet, and a blanket. There was nothing else in the room but a rolled-up canvas and an open cardboard box containing playing cards, dice, some glistening plastic implements, fancy dress, and a set of instructions.

Constance

We'll need to take those through. For when he's finished in the bathroom.

Lomas

I'm not supposed to lift heavy loads. As I explained on a previous visit, I've got a suspected inguinal hernia.

Constance

Is that really the reason, your hernia?

Lomas

Not entirely. I just don't want to help him out. I'm aware it's none of my business, but he strikes me as… he strikes me as a bit of a…

Constance

Please do tell.

Lomas

Well, let's just say he… Don't you think you could do better?

Constance

All I'm asking is you carry some bits and pieces. It's not like I'm asking you to join in.

Lomas

Is that a barbed remark?

Constance

Why should it be? Come on, get moving.

Lomas

I dragged the canvas into the lounge, where Constance busied herself unrolling it.

Constance

Aren't you going to bring the box as well?

Lomas

I saw no point in being obstructive, so I went, intending to get it, but when I was halfway to the bedroom, the toilet flushed and I had to duck back into the lounge. The canvas, I realized now, was in fact an accessory linked with the game contained in the box; on it was printed a coloured grid, the kind of grid on which a player might be arranged into comical postures while dice were rolled to determine forfeits from a list – the set of instructions in the box, or so I supposed. Constance looked flustered.

Constance

Make yourself scarce. Right now. I'll fetch the box myself. Go on, get out. God, what is *wrong* with you? Just go. And don't come back.

Lomas

I did as instructed.

11

Lomas

If I'd been called upon to justify the expenditure, I'd have found ample justification in the contents of the box file, which lent themselves freely to creative interpretation. Crump's appearance in the travel section at the library was suggestive in itself, but when you considered it in the context of the scrapes he'd got himself into, or was supposed to have got himself into, the scope for dramatic speculation became quite rich. I won't elaborate on the range of different scenarios, but you could do various things with his history of trying to help out Adele in a tight spot, and the trouble she'd had with her mother and Renton Curtis, and the business of the meathead driver whose face he'd smashed in with a wheel-lock. Extreme things happened to ordinary people all the time; gross unpleasantness was everywhere, people were hunted down for trying to do the right thing, people were hunted down for having done the wrong thing; the variations were unending. It would have been easy to use the contents of the box file as an excuse, but in fact I'd gone way beyond the stage where I needed to justify expenditure. No-one was listening – and it was good that no-one was listening. My enquiry was a muddle of obfuscations and tenuous superimpositions: Adele and Constance, the punctured eardrums and the tendency to shout, the unseen disfigurement and the foot and the game with forfeits, that whole thing of feeling easier to feel and the problem of vinegary versus biscuity, and then that whole thing with Saoirse, the sense of resentment and disgust, the putative aptitude for hatred, not to mention that whole thing about the swimming in the bay and whether I owed her something still, the swimmer suspended in the bay, or whether I owed something to my memory of the swimmer, which was different, and whether the thing that I owed, if I owed it, should take precedence over Adele and the punctured eardrums and the tendency to shout, and over Constance and the disfigurement and the foot and the game with forfeits, and over Saoirse and the scrabbling of the claw-strokes and the scuttering of the wing-bones... None of this required a hard-boiled cover story with me an earnest bounty hunter and Crump a desperate fugitive. All it required was that I walk along some cliff tops, do some work to scotch the obfuscations and superimpositions, and have a think about what to do next.

And so it was back to the old routine, the bagful of leaflets, the trudging through undesirable districts, the place in the hostel, the rented pallet, the rented pigeonhole, the incremental weekly rise in the price of staple provisions, the nightly ration of cheap whisky, the almost imperceptible swelling of the savings account, the grinding mental discomfort of the grammar drills and lists of key vocabulary in three languages, with the scrabbling of the claw-strokes and the scuttering of the wing-bones in the background – though these gradually diminished in volume and frequency, and shortly after disembarking at Calais I realized they'd pretty much ceased altogether. The fact is I got there, I was tricycling through the night and then I was tricycling into the morning, there were gulls and I could smell the stench of the sea, and then I was standing on board the ship, or sometimes sitting on board the ship, and then, as I said, the disembarkation, and with it the sudden realization that the animal noises had ceased.

Calais: a good place to begin. I could have borne right and aimed straight for the bay on the Brittany coast, but I had other, wider objectives, such as Germany, Austria, Switzerland and the northern part of Italy. My instincts told me that something useful might be revealed to me up a mountain, so the more mountains I climbed the better it would be. Of course there was nothing to say that something equally useful might not come to me in a polder, which would have meant bearing sharp left instead – the only problem being I hadn't had time to learn Dutch. There hadn't been time for Spanish or Czech or Greek or Polish or Finnish or

Bokmål or Saami either. There hadn't been time for any Chinese or Japanese, both of which I'd harboured ambitions of learning years before, as a child with an interest in calligraphy, martial arts, and noodle- and rice-based instant pot snacks.

Pouvez-vous répéter, s'il vous plaît? Können Sie das bitte wiederholen? Può ripetere, per favore? My reliance on the most basic phrasebook expedients was embarrassing; my linguistic skills were barely up to the task of buying a sandwich, let alone hunting anyone down or gaining insights into the nature of human existence. I kept remembering what Constance had said about earning lots of money, how you had to be ruthlessly strategic from the beginning, no second chances, out of your final exams and straight into the shark pool, and it seemed to me the theory worked for languages as well. I'd started too late; if I'd established myself as a polyglot by the age of twenty-one, I might have achieved a measure of influence out in the world, or at least ensured that my itinerary in Europe amounted to more than a series of trivial mortifications.

And yet my failure to communicate with speakers of other languages gave me some comfort: having no reliable notion of what was going on around me, I was effectively removed from the field of moral responsibility. Did that principle hold true for all those other things that were likely to be withheld from me forever because I'd failed to lay down the requisite skills in youth? My general lack of *savoir-faire* and *savoir-vivre,* my inability to tune in to the vernacular, all the deficiencies which had marred my enquiries to date, how dogs attacked me and cats avoided me, how most of the people I knew had ceased to exist, how there was no farmhouse in the arse-end of beyond to be converted into a den for the glugging of wine and the dousing of olives in oily infusions and the unrolling of the sex-mat three times a day, and how I'd failed to land a single brown trout from the reservoir even though I'd paid good money for the permit, and how I hadn't been able to roll my tongue or shin my way up a rope, and how I hadn't been able to whistle, and how I'd been willing to carry the mat into the lounge without the promise of a forfeit, and how I'd fallen asleep and rolled down to the bottom of the laundry pile while Saoirse was lying soapy in the bathtub: was it fair to say that failing to land the fish and not being able to roll your tongue and all the rest of it absolved you of the moral responsibility that would have come with such achievements?

Crump [box file]

As when you're sitting in a bar and then this person you know, or knew, remember knowing, saunters past and you note her slightly outdated hairstyle, overdone makeup, faded cocktail dress, and she turns to you and smiles, 'I'm drunk, yes drunk, you must be proud of me, last Christmas I started drinking and I haven't stopped drinking since, five pints of cider and I didn't know where I was, I could've been anyone's, I was drunk,' euphoric smile still fixed in place, the euphoria somehow less convincing than it was, and then her friend leads her away, her friend you also know, or knew, remember knowing, what does it matter, it matters, it bothers you, all these people must have re-emerged from somewhere, and they walk towards the bar and as they walk towards the bar you see that the cocktail dress has come undone at the back and there's the briefest glimpse of a low-slung breast from behind, a breast in eclipse, but that's OK, you have the sense that she's with decent people, honest, good-natured people, a community of drinkers who'll take care of her, they'll see her right, they'll see her home, the image of the breast in eclipse remains with you and you wander into the street, a street you recognize from years ago, it's raining, you seem to be walking through a flash flood, you linger eccentrically out in the rain, enjoying the deluge, you take shelter in somebody's door-way and that's when you notice a woman standing in the middle of the road, a woman you knew or used to know, remember knowing, she's taking the full force of the rain, she tries a few doorways and gives up, walks back to the crown of the road and stands there, resigned to her drenching, she might be laughing, you look down and see there's rainwater gushing and bubbling from the insides of your trousers, look back up and the woman is gone, you have the feeling that you're not yourself, the feeling that you haven't been yourself for several years, that you've been replicated, that someone has put an impostor in your place, that you yourself are that impostor, once the original, the authentic, now no longer, perhaps there are fifty of you, a hundred of you, each living exactly the same life as the others, equally badly, realizing only in this moment how inauthentic the whole proceeding has become, or perhaps it's merely the sky to blame, with its unhealthy, flash-flood colour, suggestive of freak atmospheric conditions and thus unnerving, nevertheless you feel an urge to discuss this matter with the woman in the cocktail dress, with her friend and with the woman in the street, and so you go back into the musty bar in the hope that they'll be waiting and quorate and ready for the debate, 'Does anyone else have the feeling that something's not quite right here?', but the moment has passed and the game has moved on and you get the sense that something beautiful and strange has been revealed to them while you were outside in the rain, there is an air of rapt serenity from which you are tacitly excluded, as a wanker in denim shorts might be excluded from a conclave of militant visionaries robing up for an evening of ecstasy, the chaste kind, or whatever it is that visionaries do in the evenings, and a woman you know, or knew, remember knowing, hands you a portable device, you look at the screen and see a hand, not hers, palm up, a blade of grass, the small of a back, a swirl of down, a crumbling leaf, an earlobe, also downed, a stone in the rain, a string of saliva, a gobbet of algae, an escarpment of pubic gooseflesh, an eye and a mouth, a different eye, a different mouth, you look more closely, the eyes look back at you with disinterest, you look more closely, the eyes look back at you with a certain self-assurance, you feel a faint sensation of loss, the woman takes back the device and says there's nothing remotely unnatural going on. 'This is just normal. You're just too late, you turned up too late. You're always too late.'

Lomas

I had a definite memory of dealing with this problem, the thing about always being too late, in a rather more comprehensive fashion during the months before my illness. A paper had been produced; it hadn't been circulated widely, but several copies had been made and stored away. I thought that a critical reassessment of that text might serve to illuminate certain matters – such as why I kept circling around things or retreating from them, while telling myself I was doing so in order to get the measure of them, and why I kept reducing people to leitmotivs and symbols, bits of facial and bodily motion, bits of hair-smell, as though collecting bits and pieces for a collage, and why, despite my genuine willingness to adapt and go on adapting, I was developing such an ominous sense of regression. It might have been useful to review the document, certainly, but a huge diversion back across the Channel would have entailed too much disruption to my plans, and I had concerns about the extra wear and tear. My anus was bunched up like a Brussels sprout and protruding, my feet hurt, my crotch was rotting, my nipples were chafed and looked like raw minced beef, and the paper in question was probably safe in some repository. I could retrieve it any time, probably. Like I said, I had my plans. I had countries to visit, mountains to go up, rivers to cross, and Romanesque churches to walk around in silence.

After I'd found the relevant bay on the Brittany coast and lain on the top of the cliff for a while and strolled up and down a few times, I decided to give the project one last shot in the form of a trip to Tadeusz Grody's. This meant a gruelling journey south to a village in Limousin, but I was up for that, in the sense that I'd been planning for it, if only as a vague eventuality, so I went, and yes, it was gruelling, but I got there, as far as the village. 'Je cherche la maison ou la ferme de monsieur Grody. Il est anglais. Pouvez-vous m'aidez?' Of the replies I received, I understood very little apart from the obvious: no-one knew Grody. But then an old soak I met in a bus shelter offered to tell me, in exchange for a swig of my brandy, something to do with an English gentle-man and his friends. The old soak in question had black fingernails and disintegrating lips, which made me reluctant to hand him the bottle, so I tipped a generous measure into the spare disposable cup I kept for emergencies and asked him to write on the back of a picture postcard what he knew. He was happy enough to oblige, and I was more than happy to let him keep the pen as well as the cup, and thus I gained the name of the house, a couple of clues to its location, and some references to what, in his opinion, had gone on there: *beaucoup de vin, beaucoup d'Anglais*, a sketch of a curved and knobbly penis scattering droplets over a bushy, gap-ing vulva and two sagging breasts.

Next day I came to it, a renovated farmhouse deep in the woods. I registered the obvious features – security gates, an in-tercom, surveillance cameras, the sweeping, gravelled drive, the luxury cars lined up in the parking bays – and didn't proceed any further. It was still a retreat, but a different sort of retreat from before: the sort of place where people in lab coats would take your money and feed a special kind of hosepipe up through your anus to flush out your guts, or rip out your pubic hair and sand-blast the mound and the crack, or give your chakra a decent fist-ing, pummelling, kneading or whatever the latest treatment was for chakras; I didn't know about the chakras to be honest, my information was out of date, I had no idea what was in vogue, I hadn't kept up with recent developments, there might be no lab coats, they might not bother with the hosepipe any more, they might even have banned it. My grasp of beauty, and how beauty liked to express itself out in the world, had lately grown weak.

Lomas [box file]

I insert this for the attention of Vulgus. I am Lomas, a jobbing clerk, a data processor, a distributor of leaflets, once an imagina-tive ethnographer, promising much, a jobbing clerk who once promised much, a glut of potential, an absence of empathy, a tendency to flinch from that which is obviously too obviously human, an accidental destroyer of souls, let's not be excessively melodramatic, a mere tormentor of souls, an accidental tormentor, let's not be excessively melodramatic, a data processor, a distributor of leaflets, once an imaginative ethnographer, seeking always to widen his orbit, in receipt of good advice from the best of people, a moral being, a genuine trier, please forgive the social clumsiness, hopeless at formal introductions, deemed it a basic professional courtesy to identify self on the off-chance, supposing you get this far, it's not beyond plausibility, there are imaginative ethnographers who remain thus, lapsing not, no jobbing clerks these, doing the work and doing it well, far better than I did, and for all I know you're one of them, but it won't do you much good, you will not find this, I hereby retract it, Vulgus won't find it.

Lomas

Nothing else for it, I'd have to make contact with Bettina, no messing around with phones or computers, a meeting in person and a confession of sorts, explicit regarding my failures and appropriately contrite, and then a return to normal duties, a normal routine, with a chance to earn some legal tender in the hope of amassing enough to secure a mortgage and buy a place or, failing that, to put down a bond on a rental property, and then try to settle down and try to live for a while, and eventually die in my sleep. As I knew too well, though, people rarely had the financial reserves to die of old age in a privately rented property; the prospect of the care home or retirement home was constantly before you, however distant it might seem, and even supposing you managed to buy a place and managed to pay off the mortgage, there was still no guarantee that one day you wouldn't head off to the bank in your pyjamas, leaving the iron plugged in and the chip pan on, and cause a scene by shitting your pants in the queue. Next thing you knew, you were watching telly in the care home with everyone else. Not that the care home or retirement home was intrinsically repulsive to me; actually I could see myself there, sitting alone in my room, by the window mainly, eking my pension out on twelve-year-old malt whisky, early classical symphonies played on period instruments, and paperback genre novels – simple pleasures, the kind I'd been denying myself for too long. The only problem was my pension: my contributions had lapsed some time ago, and twelve-year-old malt whisky didn't come cheaply. There'd be a shortfall to make up – how large was unclear, I didn't have access to the relevant documentation, so there was another wad of mouldering paper to worry about, another grubby file to be retrieved.

In short, I'd damaged my prospects. Badly.

I headed back northwards, aiming for Calais.

12

Lomas

On the other side of the Channel the scratching and knocking sounds resumed. That very first night, in the sickly-sweet warmth of a flue at the back of an overpriced service station, a desperate scrabbling penetrated my sleep, and despite what I told myself about rats in bins, and feral cats that came after rats in bins, the noises seemed so expressive of what I conjectured as Saoirse's decline and vagrancy that next morning I woke up to palpitations and dread. The noises followed me as I made my way back northwards: while I was trying to sleep in my tent, or while I was trying to get myself settled in one of the low-budget hostels I stayed in when funds permitted, that's when the noises would begin. They always started out seeming distant at first but got closer and louder the more I tried to ignore them.

One wet morning, I was cycling along and my tyres were making sizzling sounds and everything was fine until I noticed an injured blackbird in the gutter. I stopped and looked, and the blackbird looked back at me, blinking in something like bewilderment, mild bewilderment, knowing more than I could possibly know about waiting with patience to die. I blinked in return. We might have been equals if it hadn't been my superior. I would have helped it, but there was nothing I could do. The point was, I realized just how fanciful and ridiculous it had been, interpreting animal noises as commentaries on what had happened to Saoirse. It would have been just as plausible claiming that the noises had been meant to guide me *here*, to this lonely road in the sizzling wet, to witness the laudable patience and blinking of the blackbird. That was how arbitrary it was.

That night they started up again, in the form of a scratching at my tent flaps, so I switched on my torch and unzipped the flaps and peered out, and there was this mongrel dog with its tongue out and a friendly look on its face. And that was that – I mean, the noises stopped forever, two days later, once I'd rid myself of the dog. Don't misunderstand me; I'm not suggesting that the dog had been responsible for the earlier round of noises on my journey down to the Channel, that it had waited there at Dover so it could start the noises up again when I returned. I'm just saying, the noises stopped as soon as I'd rid myself of the dog. I couldn't stretch to buying dog food on top of my other living expenses, and I didn't want the extra responsibility, so I gave the dog the slip in a crowded shopping centre one day. It gave me no pleasure to be so duplicitous, but I did it, I gave it the slip. The dog wasn't Saoirse, wasn't a messenger from Saoirse, wasn't her supplicant familiar, and in any case I couldn't afford to go traipsing round the country seeking animals, blinking at animals, helping animals, in the hope of gaining some clue as to what had befallen her. The fact was, Saoirse and I could do nothing to help each other; our connection was disintegrating, just as those between Crump and his male friends and between Crump and the attestants were disintegrating, and not only those connections but the people who'd sustained them were disintegrating, as Saoirse and I were disintegrating separately, as people do if you give them enough time to do so, or as a corpse does if you put it in a bathtub full of biological washing powder. Would an underground bunker serve as protection? Were punctured eardrums symptomatic of disintegration or were they a cunning defence against it? What more had Constance lost of her living space, body mass, formerly cherished extremities? I decided to go and see her first of all.

Crump [box file]

The graves were quite peaceful. Some were overgrown, while others were lovingly tended, but all were quite peaceful. That's not a truism, by the way; I know my graves, I've seen fucking hundreds of graves in my time, and I can tell you they're not always peaceful. I've been traumatized by graves, or at least disturbed by them, especially when they've got pictures of human faces on them, faces made livid and garish by the application of blusher and pastel hues, the gravestones wearing those faces like badges, horrible badges, horrible laminated icons, worse than a shittily painted ornamental plate being flogged as a limited special edition on the back of a human interest magazine for timorous old folk or those members of the lower middle classes who still like their kitsch. That sort of image. But no, these graves were lovingly tended and quite peaceful, with no badges. Which was good. It was a relief, the distance we'd gone so we could see them.

Lomas

There was a street party underway in the communal square or courtyard. Guttural laughter, pools of vomit, streams of urine, rubbish everywhere, two naked buttocks and a vulva sticking out from the boot of a hatchback, a brawny penis hanging limply over the top of some rusty black railings, the sputter and crack of exploding fireworks, and some gunshots from a back yard. The apartment block in which Constance lived had been gutted, the interior fixtures and fittings dragged out through the holes where the doors and windows had been. Some of the debris had been heaped up to form a bonfire, not yet lit: mattresses, carpets, polystyrene, egg boxes, chipboard – all that remained, I assumed, of the ill-fated soundproofing project. To be honest, I didn't get much of a chance to scout the place that evening, as some of locals had noticed my presence and I guessed that there'd be sticks or maybe baseball bats or knives to be contended with if I stayed and looked for Constance. So I retreated. But next morning, when it was quiet, I went back again and peered in at the wreckage. No sign of Constance. Perhaps she'd thrown in her lot with the zombie from the restaurant, or with some other unsuitable man, and moved away permanently. And if Constance had thrown in her lot with an unsuitable man, Adele might have done so too, but with a different unsuitable man, such as Renton Curtis. She might have allowed him to inseminate her; even if she hadn't, she might have agreed to share a flat with him, or a house, perhaps a house that boasted a therapeutic garden round the back. I could see them planting bulbs together – charging the winter soil with the hackneyed symbolism of vernal photosynthesis. Perhaps her hearing had been restored; perhaps he'd persuaded her, ostensibly for her own good, to undergo surgery so she could listen to him talk, and now she was suffering from his neediness, his demands for meaningful confidences – an elaborate, monstrous programme of linguistic and psychological degradation, all reinforced by his facility with her fecund female relatives. How could I help her? Where to start? And what about Saoirse? We couldn't help each other, true, but still, she'd taken off all her clothes while we'd been talking, and not only that, she'd told me all about her trouble with personal pronouns. Something like that creates a bond between two people; I felt a definite obligation. But my stock of expertise was finite and shrinking. What might once have seemed like options were merely conceits. The methodology of inference, for example – that was just obfuscation and superimposition, just a conceit. I could do nothing now with the finely tuned sense of resentment or disgust, the putative aptitude for hatred; there was nothing to be inferred from them, at least nothing of practical use. And what of those little magazines in which Saoirse had published her poems, or claimed to have published her poems? A last resort, but not a viable last resort. Far too many of them, those little magazines, for me to go searching for a handful of youthful pieces by a single, obsolete author; far too many, and no doubt scattered around the world in diverse highly obscure collections, with incomplete holdings, no consolidated index, and no overarching system of formal organization. And then if I found them, there'd be nothing to apply to the findings but inference, fatuous inference; as for the body whose owner had written the things and posted them, the body that embarrassed its owner with pronouns, personal pronouns, and

whose ownership couldn't be published, all my inference would
be abject speculation: no location for that body, no global co-
ordinates, not so much as an old-fashioned grid reference, nothing at all.

Crump [box file]

We'd taken a long extended trip across the continent. It was the
last one we could afford. We didn't know that at the time, we
didn't know there'd be no more money, but that's how it goes,
it just turned out like that, the last one we could afford. And yet
we were frugal. We travelled quite cheaply. There was a river.
There was a croissant or was it a bagel or was it pretzel. There
was a river, a hut by a motorway, there was a verge and a place
to park, and even with all the cars and lorries going past, it was
somehow peaceful. There was a cemetery. No, there were cem-
eteries. We stayed in a chain of budget hotels. The chain of budget hotels was good. It's always nice to have a roof above your
head, even if that roof is just a corrugated metal roof, or was it a
kind of a flat roof, was it a felt roof, but I'll say one thing and it's
this: the linen and towels were always clean, they were spotlessly
clean. The only problem was the toilets. Yes, the toilets didn't
flush as well as they might have. It took nothing away, that flush,
it just stirred things around. You flushed, and the water came and
twirled your droppings around, and that was it. The flush just left
them bobbing about. So as I say, even though it was thunderous,
the flush, and woke everyone up, the other guests and even the
pissed-up vagrants outside, that flush just stirred your droppings
around, it took nothing away.

Lomas

Next I went to Juniper's flat. She wasn't there; a family of four,
semi-naked and copiously tattooed, appeared to have taken her
place instead. And so I went to the department store, or rather
to the site of the department store, which Juniper must have sold
for a tidy profit, whatever she claimed, and which had been

levelled so they could build flats. The flats had been built, and they'd been occupied, and some were now up for resale. And so I went back to the cottage, thinking they'd probably knocked it down too, but no, the cottage was still a cottage and if anything it looked slightly more the part of a rural cottage than before: timber window frames, thatched roof, a privet hedge trained into an archway over the gate. That said, it wasn't in good condition. It had been done up to look more rustic, yes, but then it had been allowed to lapse into dereliction again. Huge gaps in the thatching straw, front windows smashed, dark sockets in the chimney stack where bricks had flaked away, and then the front door hanging open on its sole remaining hinge, exposing bare floorboards, plaster crumbling from naked lath, and mould of various colours thriving on the walls where the plaster had held.

Juniper was sitting at a table in the back garden. She was dressed in a light summer frock. Her hand, palm down, was resting next to an oversize wine glass, just some dregs of red in the bottom, and next to the glass was a taped-up shoebox, which I guessed contained whatever was left of her cat. A scabby pigeon with half a foot missing and numerous weeping bald patches was limping about on the table, while a herring gull, scowling as herring gulls do, was stalking around her bare feet.

Juniper

Hello, you.

Lomas

Yes. Hello. It's me.

Juniper

Who's dying this time?

Lomas

I don't know.

227

Juniper

You don't?

Lomas

I don't. I'm out of touch. I've let things slip. I've come to sort things out – my pension, for example. After this, I mean. I'm off to sort my pension. Or what's left of it. I need to see some people, sort things out. You know how it is.

Juniper

Quite so. You'll need it.

Lomas

What?

Juniper

Your pension. If you live that long, you'll need it.

Lomas

Yes, that's right. And you? You're well?

Juniper

I'm pretty good, thanks. Who's dying this time?

Lomas

This time? Who was dying last time?

Juniper

What – you mean you don't remember?

Lomas

I remember you thought he was dead or maybe close to death, but...

Juniper

No. He came and told me.

Lomas

Told you?

Juniper

Yes. That he was going to.

Lomas

Oh. I'm sorry.

Juniper

You give off a lot of negative energy, like I said. That very first time, when you turned up, I knew it meant that he was dying. You were rounding people up as though they were witnesses, and questioning them, and compiling these faintly prurient little dossiers or testimonies, perhaps to be used in evidence against him, perhaps for nothing more than to rubber-stamp his death. You know how it goes. 'A book of writings shall be brought forth, a book in which all has been recorded, whence the world is to be judged.' You were a fouled-up minor clerk with a crumpled sick-note, tasked with the paragraph on Crump because it wouldn't involve much effort. After all, he hadn't done much with his life. An easy job for someone like you.

Lomas

I've never acted in that capacity.

Juniper

No, I know. I was having a joke.

Lomas

Oh. That's all right, then.

Juniper

He was clinically dead, and the people you were looking for –
me included – we were nothing more than figments of his disintegrating consciousness. His mind, you see, had invented us – you
included – so we could help him unlock some final piece of vital
information before the neurons, what was left of them, extin-
guished themselves for good. And once we'd revealed it, once
he'd made whatever peace he needed to make with himself, he'd
slip away into nothingness forever. Just like he wanted.

Lomas

How many more of these jokes have you got?

Juniper

I know what you thought of me back then. A daft old hippie, full
of woolly-minded ideas knocked off from new-age spirituality
forums and farting sessions on yoga mats in church halls. I'm only
living up to the stereotype. You can't deny me the chance to have
a bit of fun at your expense.

Lomas

Whatever you say.

Juniper

You really think I might have believed myself the figment of
someone's disintegrating consciousness?

Lomas

I didn't say you did.

Juniper

Well, good. Because, you know, I'm here. See? I can feel myself
and everything. And Crump was never a solipsist. If he were
here, I'm sure he'd be able to feel me too.

Lomas

And you'd let him?

Juniper

Yes. And last time I saw him, he did. And yes, I let him.

Lomas

The time he told you he was dying?

Juniper

He looked so bad, he almost didn't have to say. I could see that he was done for. He'd been trying to fail with dignity, but he'd failed at even that. I suppose he'd wanted to slip through the everyday fault lines and go on existing in some kind of dream-life, soused in alcohol and grinning at the shadows, no human connections, no possessions but what he could pack into a rucksack or a small trunk, no mortgage or tenancy agreement, no crushing sense of eternal commitment, no more of the vomit-inducing terror that comes from contemplating mutual confinement forever, or at least until the first death. But what he found instead was homelessness, the banality of homelessness, nothing more.

Lomas

Sleeping rough, it's not the best thing for your health.

Juniper

I know. He was living on the streets when he discovered that he was dying.

Lomas

What was he dying of?

Juniper

Old age.

231

Lomas

You're sure of that?

Juniper

That's what he told me. I said Jesus you look dreadful, and he said yes, old age is dreadful, then he told me. He'd been having this recurring dream, and in this dream he started off asleep, and when he woke up he found three decades had passed overnight. He kept on having it, this dream; and then one morning he woke up and it was true, three decades had passed overnight, he was seventy-five and soon he was going to die. That's why he landed on my doorstep, looking dreadful. He had this urge to make his apologies, make his peace, before he died.

Lomas

And this was when?

Juniper

Just after you moved out of the storeroom. It wasn't convenient, to be honest, the way he appeared like that without warning. I had a guest at the flat and plans to make, and also I was busy concluding the sale of the department store with the buyers, which hadn't gone smoothly. I mean, it's not like I was expecting it to go smoothly – that kind of business never does – but I was inured to it, and dealing with the stress of it, and suddenly there's this wastrel from my past, and he's demanding absolution or forgiveness or whatever, on the doorstep of my flat. And he's turned seventy-five overnight, or at least he's telling me he's turned seventy-five overnight. What's up? You look like you're in pain.

Lomas

I'm just a little bit disappointed on behalf of his friends and admirers. You know, to learn that his achievements as a philosopher should have ended with a parable about waking up to find he's aged three decades overnight. At least, I'm assuming it's a parable.

Juniper

What do you mean?

Lomas

I mean a parable by Crump, and not another one of your jokes.

Juniper

No need to get shirty. I'm just telling you what he said.

Lomas

Then perhaps we should leave it there.

Juniper

You mean to dismiss him just like that?

Lomas

I'm not dismissing him. I just think we should leave it there, and maybe talk about the others.

Juniper

Others?

Lomas

Yes. Adele, for instance.

Juniper

Why Adele?

Lomas

Don't know. Perhaps it's none of my business. I just feel I should have followed up my last visit with another. Taken some medical pamphlets and urged her to see a doctor.

233

Juniper

What was wrong with her?

Lomas

Her ears. There was something wrong with her ears.

Juniper

When was this?

Lomas

While I was staying in your storeroom. She was living underground in a kind of chamber. There was something wrong with her ears. But it's not just Adele. There's Saoirse, too. It's just a feeling I've got. A sense I could have conducted myself with greater aplomb or propriety. For a start, I really shouldn't have taken her car.

Juniper

Her car?

Lomas

That's right, I took her car. But it was someone else who stole it. Then there's Constance. I could have handled things better with Constance.

Juniper

You're just like Crump. This is what he did. Turning up like that, all penitence and remorse but keeping the lion's share of his penitence and remorse for all the others. Hello Juniper, sorry for fucking around or licking around or being sucked off or whatever it was I got up to round about the time I abandoned you, but I need to make amends before I cop it. Next thing I'm making some excuse and my guest is packing and we're trying to find a decent hotel at short notice so that Crump can dump his stuff and have the beanbags.

Lomas

I can see it must have rankled.

Juniper

Then, when he's got what he wanted, he's off to see the others. What am I meant to make of that? A further betrayal? A final insult?

Lomas

As I say, it must have rankled.

Juniper

Rankled. Quite.

Lomas

The herring gull flapped its wings, rose up, and landed clumsily on the table, putting the pigeon to panicky flight. A jettisoned feather tumbled slowly across the table top, and a gobbet of green-and-white shit slid down the inside of Juniper's glass. *Columba livia.*

Juniper

Since you mention it, I actually thought he was trying to do the right thing. And who can say? Perhaps he had a premonition. You know – like I had, about him.

Lomas

A premonition?

Juniper

To do with them dying. Or being about to die – quite soon.

Lomas

And are they?

Juniper

Are they? Don't you mean were they?

Lomas

All right. Were they?

Juniper

How should I know? And why tell you? What do you think is going on here? You want to be spoon-fed, you think I'm a night-nurse in suspenders, you want me to wipe your bum and pat your itchy scrotum down with talc and clean your face with a hanky I've spat in?

Lomas

It'd be easier.

Juniper

Christ. They don't half send me some pricks.

Lomas

Her fingers had tightened around the stem of the oversize wine glass, and her expression had hardened. Nothing to be inferred from that, the tightening, the hardening; I took the decision not to infer, and I stuck to it. A tightening, a hardening. A woman with a slightly hardened face.

Juniper

Saoirse – dead. That's for certain. End-stage liver disease. She got herself in the papers. Died in a car crash. Took the car of a friend or acquaintance without consent, and then she drove it into a tree. Or was it a wall. Forget which. Anyway, she finished herself off before her liver got the chance to do it for her. Sad, but hardly unexpected.

Lomas

What about Constance?

Juniper

Possibly dead. I don't keep a scrapbook. There was this rumour to do with some terrible sort of hiking accident, tragic, in the snow.

Lomas

The snow?

Juniper

In Finland. Northern Finland. Where she was hiking.

Lomas

And Adele?

Juniper

I've no idea.

Lomas

Not even a rumour?

Juniper

Not even a rumour.

Lomas

She relaxed her grip on the wine glass and extended her hand to tickle the herring gull's breast. Herring gull. *Larus argentatus.* Looking quite cross, as herring gulls do, it snapped at her fingers. Then it flew off.

Juniper

Poor Adele. She was just a disaster.

Lomas

After I'd finished speaking to Juniper, I went and did what I said I was going to do, I tried to sort out my pension and see about the paper I'd produced on the question of always being too late. Back in the days before the project, when I'd been building up to having a life or whatever you want to call it, I'd paid a lump sum in advance for a safe deposit box — fifty years the initial term, with the option to renew. I had the feeling that the document about always being too late was in there somewhere — I'd added various bits and pieces while I'd been working with Bettina — so I went to the counter and spoke to the man and he brought me the box and I spent a couple of hours going through it. And yes, the document was there, but it was little more than a short account of a man who'd chosen to spend some time in a bar, and then in the street, and then in the bar again. As when a person you vaguely remember walks past your table, you note her slightly outdated hairstyle, overdone makeup, faded cocktail dress, she turns to you and smiles, the boozy confession, the smiley euphoria, the glimpse of the low-slung breast, the street you recognize from years ago, the flash flood, somebody's doorway, the woman standing in the middle of the road, the rainwater gushing from the insides of your trousers, the feeling you haven't been yourself for several years, that you've been replicated, that someone has put an impostor in your place, that you yourself are that impostor, the urge to discuss it, the woman, the portable device, the hand palm up, the blade of grass, the small of the back, the swirl of down, the crumbling leaf, the earlobe, the stone in the rain, the string of saliva, the gobbet of algae, the eyes, the mouths, the faint sensation of loss, the statement of fact about always being too late.

The only significant difference from Crump's account consisted in the names. Because I'd given the people names. And Crump, he hadn't.

Crump [box file]

In fact I was disappointed generally by continental toileting. I'd heard a great deal about it, but none of my preconceptions really held true. Take inspection ledges for droppings, for example. I'd heard a great deal about inspection ledges for droppings, but once I was out there not a single ledge for droppings did I see. As for bidets, I was disappointed by bidets most of all. Perhaps I'd been deluding myself, or not listening properly, or someone had played a joke on me as a child; however you look at it, I was deceived. I'd always assumed, you see, that the bidet introduced a jet of clean water into the anus so you didn't have to scrape at your anus with paper and get a sore anus. But that wasn't necessarily true, as I discovered when I encountered one. A bathroom in a cheap hotel, not part of the chain I mentioned, just a cheap hotel, quite shabby, and actually dirty when I think about it in detail, and there was this bidet. And I'd been expecting a sort of toilet with a fixture that spurted some water up at your anus, but this was more like a kind of sink, a knee-high sink with a couple of taps. You were meant, I suppose, to fill it with water and sit and let the water lap at your hole. No high-pressure jet. Almost not worth the bother of making the things. The hotel with the bidet was in the same city as the cemetery, I believe.

Lomas

I thought I'd probably still have access to the archive in the building where we'd worked together, Bettina and I, though it struck me that I might have to fill out some forms and maybe sit for an hour in reception while they did me a new ID card or a visitor's pass or something. That's how it is when you're a feckless returner, a peripatetic redundant, an emeritus clerk of bad works and public nuisances for a day; you just have to yield to whatever procedural obligations they impose on you, and smile, and let them know you know they're doing you a favour. And it's true that I didn't have anywhere else to be that day, no other important business affairs demanding my urgent attention. I was focused on the task in hand, the digging out of the document, be it duplicate or variant, for comparison with the one in the safe deposit box, and also there was finding out exactly what had happened with Bettina, what her status was, or, if she had no status, where I might be able to reach her.

At reception they asked me to prove that I was the person I claimed to be, and once I'd done so, Paul, an Assistant Outreach Liaison Manager, came along to liaise with me. I told him I'd like to see whatever they had for me, or on me, in the stacks downstairs in the basement – assuming they still had stacks in the basement – filed by surname, under Lomas. This seemed to throw him, but we started walking anyway, in the direction of the stairs. As we walked, I saw that the layout had changed quite radically, though I recognized one of the rooms we passed as Bettina's former office – now converted into a meeting room and furnished with low-profile coffee tables and brightly coloured beanbags. I asked young Paul how long it had been since Bettina had moved out from that room, but it transpired that he was new to the post and wasn't aware of anyone in the service, either now or in the recent past, with a name like that, Bettina. Was that French, or maybe German? I suggested he refer me to an older colleague – perhaps someone in estates, or maybe a secretary, if they still employed older secretaries – who might be able to remember some of the staff from further back than the recent past, and while he was phoning for authorization I wandered off and made my own way down to the basement, where a man in yellow overalls and a high-visibility jacket intercepted me. He was wearing a brushed steel badge, and this badge identified him as Claudio. He offered to help, so I said I was looking for the storeroom where the effects of lapsed employees and former visitors were held.

Claudio

The glory hole?

Lomas

Possibly. There'll be boxes there, pending late collection or post-humous disposal.

Claudio

That's the glory hole all right. This way please, mate.

Lomas

He didn't ask for authorization. Maybe he thought I was somebody else.

Claudio

Mate, you look terrible. Really terrible. What's with that, then?

Lomas

For want of something better to say, I told him the one about the bloke who dreams he's aged three decades overnight and then he wakes up and he finds he's aged three decades overnight. What Claudio made of it I don't know, but it seemed to intrigue him, prompting various reflections on how strange life was, or could be, along with various facts, or approximations to fact, which he recalled from scientific documentaries he'd seen years ago, on neurological aspects of sleep and dreaming, and on time perception in humans and other animals. As he was chuntering away, I found the box I wanted, and started to glance through its contents.

Claudio

No, but really, mate. You look trashed.

Lomas

I had to post leaflets for a living. And then there were times I had to sleep behind a hedge.

Claudio

You're taking that with you?

Lomas

Yes, it's worthless. And it's taking up valuable space.

Claudio

Right you are, mate. Should be fine. Just need to check it against the register.

Lomas

Checking against the register took several minutes, which seemed excessively long for what the process entailed, and as I waited I began to feel uneasy. I kept expecting him to mention someone called Vulgus, a query from Vulgus, red flag placed against the file in the name of Vulgus, unlimited access requested by Vulgus, please sign here to grant permission in perpetuity to Vulgus. It wasn't implausible as an outcome. In the event, though, there was no such complication. There was just Claudio, staring down his nose at a portable device which he clearly held in low esteem, a source of daily vexation and dubious veracity. Still, I was curious, and I felt like chancing my luck – or, if not luck, whatever it was that had got me this far. At this late juncture in my career, I could afford to live a bit dangerously, I thought, and so I asked him if he knew a researcher called Vulgus.

Claudio

Researcher?

Lomas

Yes. Researcher called Vulgus.

Claudio

Vulgus? No.

Lomas

You don't remember him? We're going some way back here.

Claudio

Don't remember him.

Lomas

Bettina?

Claudio

What about her?

Lomas

You remember her? Bettina?

Claudio

Absolutely. Couldn't forget her. Lovely woman. Magnificent woman. Terrible, it was, the way she went.

Lomas

The way she went?

Claudio

Before she died. I mean, passed away. The way she was treated. Bloody disgraceful, it was, and no-one called to account for it.

Lomas

There was a question of culpability? Unresolved?

Claudio

You're telling me.

Lomas

A question of negligence?

Claudio

Right. Of negligence. Question. Exactly.

Lomas

There was a clear miscarriage of justice?

Claudio

They spread rumours, and they damaged her reputation.

Lomas

Surely she fought it. Surely she gave as good as she got.

Claudio

She was ill at the time. She couldn't give her undivided attention
to the case.

Lomas

Is there a rear exit here? A way out to the loading bay?

Claudio

What for?

Lomas

Carrying boxes through reception areas generally makes me
puke. With people looking. Is there a rear exit here? A way out
to the loading bay?

Claudio

Round there, mate. Down the corridor. Then turn left.

Lomas

Despite his instructions, I briefly got lost. When I emerged from
the basement corridors into the loading bay, I opened the box
and read.

Crump [box file]

It was a pilgrimage of sorts, a secular pilgrimage. Which is a dismal way to put it, and a dismal thing to admit to. But I wanted to go, I felt an obligation to go, to see where they'd laid him to rest. I thought it right that I pay my respects to a man whose work I admired, a man unjustly neglected while alive. And so I found the grave and I stood there, thinking, reflecting. It was quite formless, the way I was thinking or reflecting, but there was one thing that impressed itself on me clearly and rather forcibly, and that was the size of the grave, the size of the plot, which seemed too small for a human body. Everyone says that, I suppose, about any grave going, unless the heirs or the local choral society have gone to town with a bloody great mausoleum – which, in this case, no-one had. There was a memorial in black marble, but the plot itself was small, remarkably small. And there was silence. And in that silence, for just a brief moment, I heard the universe resounding. It was resounding in his compositional style, which critics in liner notes would often describe as 'bleak', or 'lunar', or 'glacial'. And the tone of this resounding, which didn't strike me at all as 'bleak' or 'lunar' or 'glacial', made me think about his brain, and what had happened to his brain, which didn't exist any more, and when or at what point a thing like consciousness might be said to cease to exist, and how long an instant was, or eternity was, when viewed from the perspective of fading neurons. It wasn't my area, didn't interest me, never had. Of course I knew about the theories, popular theories. Such as eternal life may be said to exist in the sense that the region or regions of the brain in which awareness of self and/or memory and/or consciousness is/are seen to be located is/are terminally abstracted from linear time at the moment of death, and that which is terminally abstracted from linear time is necessarily incapable of registering the transience of its condition and may therefore be said to form a closed system which, internally, exists in what is effectively a state of perpetuity, of eternity. Theories like that. They didn't interest me, as I said. It was unpleasant enough to have such a place as a graveyard where you could go and imagine it happening, down in the soil, just stand there thinking about the crumbling unaware of its own crumbling and the fading unaware of its own fading after the brain has rotted away. Whatever you think about the theory, the standing there thinking is quite unpleasant, and in a sense it's quite indecent to try to believe or try to disbelieve the theory. That's how I felt: indecent to speculate. The ethics of graveyard tourism, they're a minefield.

Lomas

As I expected, all it said was what the other paper, the one in the safe deposit box, had said. The grammar was tighter, in the narrow sense of being more prescriptive, but the essence was the same.

It all had something to do with Bettina. Not in the obvious way. In the obvious way, it had nothing to with Bettina. When I thought about Bettina I got so far with it, and when I thought about the attestants I got so far with it, but every time I got anywhere close to isolating the issue, what came up was a meaningless blank. So in the way of further analysis stood Bettina, and in the way of further analysis stood the attestants, and so it followed that in the way of further analysis stood what had brought me to the point where further analysis had been theoretically possible. It therefore followed that I'd come to the end of all knowledge, of what I was capable of knowing, which didn't seem much.

I am too old for this, too confused and need to stop trying so hard to think. It doesn't suit me. Not a good thinker. Not in that way.

Crump [box file]

And the ghoulishness of it. Prowling around and peering. And not only that, you've got the hierarchy of souls to think about too. Whose grave to make for on arrival? Whose grave drops first off the list when you fancy a coffee or your feet begin to get sore? There was another composer buried in the same cemetery – an inferior talent, certainly, but not without appeal, and more successful in his own lifetime than the one I admired so greatly – and as I stood before his mausoleum, I found myself unable to recall a single bar of what he'd written. This made me feel guilty and disrespectful. But when I reflected on it, I realized that I was wrong to feel like that. It was a kindness, in a way, to forget his work, or the majority of it; benevolent in the extreme to be the agent of amnesia when it came to the more banal pieces, of which, I'm sorry to say, he wrote quite a lot. So I was doing him a favour, saving his blushes, preserving his modesty.

None of which served to excuse my neglect of the others. All the others. I just passed them by, the graves of the people whose works had failed to survive, or which had never got round to existing. They'd made good cabinets in that region; you still saw lots of them in antique shops; maybe some of the graves contained the remains of cabinetmakers. And surely there'd be plenty of diarists interred there; statistically it was likely that a few of them would have been seriously talented, while even the less accomplished would have had interesting things to say about their lives; perhaps there were one or two diaries extant, in boxes or files somewhere, to prove it. If so, it wasn't my business to read them. It was bad enough reading the diaries and correspondence of the composers you admired. No-one's business, all the dreck that they imprudently failed to destroy.

Lomas

What next, follow Crump's example, make my peace with the attestants, all of them dead except for Juniper, would she be sitting at the table, would her hair be encrusted with guano, did she have any hair, should I seek out the graves of the others, should I fail to speak with conviction, should I fail to speak to the dead as I had failed to speak to the living, I mean should I fail to speak with conviction, should I make my peace with Juniper, how should I make my peace with Juniper when there was nothing left to be said, when there was nothing to be done, not with the hand palm up, the small of the back, the earlobe, the string of saliva, the eye, the mouth, the hairy old undercarriage, the mouth.

Perhaps she'd started to smell of stale urine. Perhaps I'd lose control of my sphincter. Perhaps my bowel would descend into my scrotum.

And I was thinking again about Vulgus. There was a sense I had of moral obligation, at the root of which was pity. What could you do to help a poor deluded fool, whoever he was, when he'd chosen to stake his life on a wad of rejectamenta, another fool's leavings, and not only that, but yet another fool's enlargements on, and addenda to, the leavings of the first, what was it, his 'exegetical commentary', sheer pornography I'd call it, intimate details about the lives of those who hadn't been consulted, no-one had asked them, I mean the business of disseminating the findings, no-one had asked them, what did I call them, the attestants, no-one had canvassed their views on disseminating the findings, and there was that other bad business, the litter of crass incidentals, all the way through, the stinking rubbish trail of compromising irrelevancies, the autobiographical references, the allusion to the peevishness of the prose before the illness, then the memory of the bay with the swimmer who swam, the wavelets, the scales of dead fish, the not-moving, the making-no-progress, the being suspended in the middle of the bay, all of which showed me in an unflattering and a negative and a culpable light while setting out no framework, valid or otherwise, for researchers, future researchers, Vulgus and other future researchers, no advice on interpretation, what in the world had I been thinking of, and thinking with, and what in the end were you left with, what could you leave him and the others, were you to leave it, but I'd made my peace with posterity, that is with Vulgus, as you'll have seen, if you exist, whoever you are, I'd left my disclaimer, taken it out and then decided to put it back in again. Even so, to the casual reader it must seem that most of my life had been devoted to a prurient interest in things, affairs, that didn't truly concern me.

It's not unexpected, but it's odd, how painfully thin the air has become. And how much space there is around the thing, the pinnacle here, I crouch on, where there isn't room to lie down. The fear of haemorrhoids – because of the surface, which is concrete. Hug your knees. Don't rock too hard or you'll tip yourself off, and there will be falling, there will be guts, and there will be brain-stuff spattered about.

Just an image, that. Not a real pinnacle. Not a real surface.

Fear of haemorrhoids.

She said something cutting before I left. You think you've lived well, you think that because you haven't done harm, excessive harm, to other people, you must have lived well. But you haven't lived well. Your life has been less of a life than a dodgy feasibility study for life. Someone else could have lived it. You haven't. You haven't lived well.

I put it another way. I'd been noncommittal, yes, I'd failed to intervene when it mattered, on the whole I'd given little, but conversely I had taken almost nothing, and in doing so I had done myself no good – which hardly counted as self-sacrifice, but which wasn't exactly a bad way to conduct yourself, and which therefore might be construed as living well.

She wasn't convinced. Neither was I. What she'd said was vaguely perceptive. I probably hadn't.

But I'd learned some lists of names, in English and Latin. That is, I could name some birds and lichens.

And I'd learned to say 'I do not understand' and 'Can you repeat that, please?' in several western European languages.

And when it was time to go and I went, there might be a blackbird in the grass. I'd want to feed it, but I wouldn't have any seed, I probably wouldn't have any money to spend on seed, you went to a garden centre and bought it, or to a hardware shop, or a pet shop, that's where you bought it. But there'd be a blackbird, there might be a blackbird, in the grass. I'd be able to see it – if it were there. *Turdus merula*. That is a blackbird. *Turdus merula*. I have lived well.